Murder for Short

Cozy Murders

Short Stories

S h i r l e y   M a s o n

Mason Publishing
Green Valley, Arizona

Also by Shirley Mason

Five Couples

The Cav Neumont Saga

The Strength of Water

The Strength of Time

The Strength of Love

The Strength of Mercy

In progress

Send Help, short stories

Eight cozy murders. Each with a different kind of detective trying to find comfort in, and solutions to his own life, while tracking a devious and scheming murderer. Sometimes with success, sometimes without.

Disclaimer

Each of these eight murder mystery short stories is fiction. Names, characters, places, and incidents either are the product of the author's imagination or are used fictitiously. Any resemblance to actual persons, living or dead, events, or locales is entirely coincidental.

Contents

The Hand at the Top of the Stairs   *1*

Death Deals a Blow at Spangle Dangle Specialties   *32*

The Mysterious Death of Lady Harrod   *55*

A Murder on Rolling Rock Road   *84*

The Green Valley Painting Club Murder   *104*

A Naturopathic Death   *124*

Chef Able Kookum Goes Down   *145*

A Murder at Canyon Grove Retirement Residence   *172*

About the author   *222*

Murder for Short

Eight cozy murders

The Hand at the Top of the Stairs

Meryl Tyson, of Tyson Realty, started up the back stairs of Goldbrick Mansion. With thirty-nine rooms, not including eight bathrooms and five staircases, it was easy to be lost—and she was lost. Confused. She had taken a wrong turn while touring the mansion. She wished she had not left the group. She couldn't even hear them. Maybe they were still upstairs, but she had just come from there. Somehow, they had become separated. She could hear a kitty crying. Holding onto the banister, she went up three steps. Her purple platform heels, meant to look sexy and catch

Glen's eye, had not been the best choice for a real-estate broker on a home tour.

Distracted, she was thinking about Glen's sexy glances, when she noticed something out of place at the top of the stairs. A hand? Could that be a hand? A red hand draped over the top step? Terror made her stomach turn. She stopped and held on to the banister for support. It was a hand. What was it doing there? Her mind refused to be logical. A jeweled hand. A red jeweled hand. And making it red—.

Blood.

Should she continue up she wondered. She stepped up slowly, just far enough to see the body attached to the hand. A woman, familiar, blonde hair spread out and sticky with red stuff. Blood all over the hardwood floor around her and smeared onto the blue and gold Persian carpet. Meryl stood stunned—determined not to go up one more step. She had to get help. She had to go down where there was some life. Not be alone. She thought of 911, and with a trembling hand, reached in her shoulder bag for her remote. She dialed 911 and stammered out that there was an emergency at Eight North Lane, East Hampton. A body on an upper back hall. She would try to find her way to the front door to lead the EMT's to the body—if she could find it again. She needed bread crumbs. Well, that *could* have been funny, she thought.

When Detective Andrew McRae, known to his friends and to Flicker, his cat, as 'Andy,' got the call to go to Eight North Lane, he was brushing Flicker, so named because of his tail. Flicker's job was to purr loudly, and he did; could be heard across the room. Flicker thought he was providing interesting occupation for Andy, whereas, Andy thought he was accumulating loose cat hair. One action, two benefits. With his tail, Flicker could register "yes," "no," "maybe," or "that's boring." Andy was attempting to move passed "that's boring" when the telephone rang. Flicker, the eternally shedding cat, a hair manufactory, gave a "no" tail flick and looked at Andy with dismay. Brushing was over for now.

Andy looked at his mobile and saw the call was from headquarters. He listened and jotted down some hieroglyphics that Flicker stared at knowingly.

"Sorry, Pal. Duty calls . . . those who give us the money to buy kibbles. I have to go. You be a good kitty and guard the place. I'll be back later. And our favorite woman will be here for dinner with us. That is if I can make it back in time."

He put fresh water and kibbles into sparkling clean, white china dishes and set them down on Flicker's dinner mat. He had already showered and dressed, and now he strapped on his gun holster and pulled on a warm jacket. Winter was hanging on, not yet ready to yield to Spring. He pocketed his mobile, a notebook, pen, and vinyl gloves, and gave Flicker a parting touch.

Number Eight North Lane, a mansion, had just been placed on the market and Glen Chapman, broker extraordinaire with Tyson Realty, had landed the listing. Seems he had some kind of *in* with the mansion owner, Susan King. The salespersons in Tyson Realty wondered how Glen won that *primo* listing. Nan Newby was particularly upset about it because Susan King was her first cousin, and Nan had half hoped to get the listing. Glen was quiet on the topic.

Tyson Realty salespeople were: Meryl Tyson, the owner of the firm; sales agents Tipper Thorpe, Nan Newby, and Glen Chapman. Glen could sell anything. He could sell a house that was regularly flooded during heavy rain. He had shown a video of a dinghy being rowed through a downstairs window . . . and still sold the house to the people who saw the video.

Today was the day the brokers were to have their first look at Goldbrick Mansion. Yesterday, in her stiff, self-important demeanor, Susan had sat in Tyson's office and signed the listing contract. Glen Chapman led the meeting. Meryl observed that he and Susan seemed to know each other quite well; looks passed between them. Meaningful looks. Meryl sucked in her breath and bit her lip. Maybe it's nothing, but it might also be what she'd suspected all along.

After Susan left the office, Meryl asked Glen, "How long have you known Susan?"

"Oh, not long. I barely know her. She belongs to my country club. I give her a thrill Friday nights and dance with her. Her husband died last year and she comes to the club alone."

Meryl wondered what other thrills he may have given Susan. Meryl had a particular arrangement with Glen that she did not want to lose. He took care of her personal needs—aside from those of Tyson Realty—in return for which he was able to keep most of the commissions he earned through sales. A profitable swap of benefits that Glen did not want to ruin. This, of course, was an arrangement unknown to Tipper and Nan.

When Detective McRae arrived at Eight North Lane, crime scene tape had already been placed across the driveways, front and back, and police vehicles cluttered the extensive grounds. Radios and chatter blared from all directions. With the help of police stationed along the halls to direct people, McRae found his way through the massive structure and upstairs to the crime scene. Technicians had already begun dusting for fingerprints, and that would take days, considering the size of the building. McRae took a few digital photos of the body and jotted down his preliminary findings. Susan King had been struck on the right side of her head by what appeared to have been a hard, sharp-edged object, which had not yet been found. Judging from the blood smears, she had tried to drag herself to the banister, perhaps to pull herself up, and there she drew her last breath, her hand falling over the stair edge.

Satisfied for the time being, McRae wandered the upper hallway looking for the way downstairs to the kitchen. He had asked the police to require those who were in the house when the body was discovered, to meet him there. When he found the kitchen, the four Tyson employees were waiting, seated at a long, thick and clear, glass bar, which formed a semi-circular island in the enormous room. Outfitted in blue blazers with gold Tyson Realty emblems and khaki skirts or trousers, they looked to McRae like sailors on their way to a local yacht club regatta. He slid onto a bar stool opposite the four agents, and showed his badge as he nodded his hellos. They stared at him. His entry had caused them to stop their chatter, and he knew they could have agreed on a story. That was okay. He could always get to the truth. He sensed anger. What would they have to be angry about? While they introduced themselves around, he studied them—jittery, he thought, and Mr. Chapman's eyes were swollen and red. Was that from grief?

"I couldn't have killed her, detective," Meryl Tyson jumped in without being asked. "When I went through the house Tipper and Nan were right behind me."

Nan gave her a look.

"Except for Nan," Meryl continued, "who just got her license and joined the office this week, we've all been with Tyson Realty many years. Tyson agents have a sterling reputation." A thin, wiry woman with a harsh, blonde bob that hung down in points around her face, Meryl Tyson looked uncomfortable and kept adjusting her blazer.

The detective focused a blank look at her, but gave no reply.

"Together we moved quickly through the house, as we had another house to review this afternoon," she said. "Glen didn't tour with us and was already waiting in the kitchen when we staggered in. We had agreed beforehand to meet in the kitchen after viewing the mansion so we could compare notes. But when I saw the body . . ." she stopped to suppress a gasp, "it was horrible and I called 911. Then with difficulty, I found my way to the front to wait for the ambulance. What a mansion! This fatality is most unfortunate. Our office felt so proud to land this important listing. With the market down and sales off right now, we're all eager to have some income. And I was the one who had to tell the others that something had happened to Susan."

She seemed to have quickly recovered from her shock, McRae thought. He wondered if her position as owner of Tyson Realty caused her to be the group spokesperson. Or was tension the cause of her yatter? He wrote something in his notebook.

"Did you *stay* together?" asked McRae.

"Yes," Meryl said, "except for Glen."

"Well, actually . . ." butt in Nan, "we split up." She looked at Meryl. "There were just too many directions to go in. Too much to marvel at, and we got separated."

Meryl pressed her mouth tightly into a slit and looked through the glass bar down at the floor. "Oh, yes, and a few minutes later I heard you and Susan yelling; having a heated argument."

"What was that about?" McRae asked Nan.

"I unexpectedly bumped into Susan sitting in her bedroom. That was the first I knew that she was home . . . she wasn't supposed to be. I told her that as we were cousins, I had hoped to get the listing, and she yelled at me that she was free to do as she wished. I was getting nowhere. Frustrated, I left her sitting at her desk."

"Did you expect Susan to be home?" Detective McRae asked the group.

Simultaneously, Meryl said *no*, and Glen said *yes*—then wished he had said nothing. Now he had to think fast.

"Which is it?" Detective McRae asked, looking from Meryl to Glen, and back.

"Normally, during a home tour, the owner finds it more comfortable to be out," Meryl said. "Susan had said she wouldn't be home for our inspection. So, we let ourselves in. This was an exclusive listing for Tyson Realty. Susan didn't want other brokers to show the mansion unless accompanied by one of us, so she had given each of us a key."

"Why did you say *yes*, Mr. Chapman?" McRae asked.

"Well . . . ," Glen stuttered, "ah . . . I saw her car in the garage." That he had slept at the mansion wasn't their business, he said to himself.

"Wouldn't you have expected numerous servants, to be here, a house this size?" Detective McRae asked the group.

"No," Meryl said. "Susan told us that since her husband died, she had been supporting the mansion on a shoestring, could only afford one housekeeper, and as that woman had retired and moved to Florida to be near her brother, Susan had picked this convenient time to list the estate for sale."

"Can any of you think of a reason Ms King might be assaulted right after listing with your agency?" McRae asked.

No one volunteered a reply.

Detective McRae shifted around on the stool and scratched his cheek abstractedly. He waited, tapping his pen on the glass. What a huge slab of glass, he thought. It had to be four inches thick. He fingered the thick, smooth, rounded edge. This appeared to be a cue for the agents to relax and they seemed to uncoil.

Solidly built with piercing eyes, Detective McRae was an intimidating authority figure— well used to solving crimes. His strong points were in watching and listening carefully—not missing details. And now he could hear a kitty crying. He tried to stay focused on the interrogation, but the cry was distracting. Finally, he asked, "Is there a cat in the house?"

"Ah . . . yes. Ah . . . I don't know, but I hear one . . . I think," Glen said. He didn't know what to do, or what to say. Was there a cat? What was this detective saying? Try to think who could have hurt Susan. He must try not to fall apart, but his mind kept racing back over what had just happened. He had been working in his office, the one Susan had let him use, and he had been thinking that it would soon be time to go down to the kitchen and wait for the Tyson bunch. He had to beat them down there—it wouldn't do to let Meryl learn that he had an office here. Then he had heard sirens. Loud sirens. Sirens coming to the manor. Thinking back, he remembered, that he had heard a funny loud thump—but he had brushed it aside; the brokers were no doubt already going through the house. They probably knocked over something, Susan had been planning to go out shopping and had probably left by now. He had hurried on down to the kitchen to wait for the others—find out what the sirens were about. It was in the kitchen that he had learned, when Meryl got there, that something had happened to Susan. In a panic, he had started back up to find her. He was stopped by the police, who by now had blocked off the crime scene.

"Go back to the kitchen," the policeman had said. "You must wait in the kitchen . . . Detective McRae will join you there."

But Glen shoved the policeman and yelled, "I have to find Susan."

"Sir, there's been an accident. You must wait in the kitchen with the others. EMT's are upstairs taking care of the victim."

Trying to keep control, Glen thought it would probably be wise to do as the man said and he turned and stumbled back to the kitchen. With some effort to concentrate, he pulled himself up on a bar stool, intent on ignoring the others' stares, intent on trying to remain sane while he waited with the others for Detective McRae.

But now it was proving nearly impossible to think about what this detective was saying.

McRae wanted to set aside the crying cat for the moment and stay focused. He asked the pertinent question again, phrasing it differently: "Could there be a connection between Ms King's selling the mansion and a reason to attack her?"

"Since Nan is Susan's cousin," Meryl said, "maybe Nan can tell you something about Susan's enemies." She directed a look over to Nan.

"But Susan and I hardly knew each other," Nan said. "She was from the wealthy side of the family and I from the poor cousins, as it were. She ignored us. I don't know who her friends or enemies are . . . or were.

"But, Nan," Meryl said, "when we heard that she was going to sell, and you mentioned that she was your cousin, you seemed to expect her to sign with you."

Nan glared at Meryl. "When I heard through family gossip that Susan would be moving, I did call her for the listing." She cast a rueful glance toward Glen.

Glen shrugged his shoulders.

"Ms Tyson, you said you stayed together, but weren't you alone when you found the body . . . when you called 911?" Detective McRae asked Meryl.

"Yes, that's true. Except for Glen, we stayed together. However, with so much distraction, I forgot that I had accidentally left a folder of listings somewhere. I wanted to back up and find the folder but I wandered around lost. Soon, I thought that perhaps Tipper and Nan had gone downstairs so I found a stairway, went down, and was still lost. This mansion has a confusing array of stairs and halls. Eventually I found myself at the bottom of a back staircase. Then I thought maybe my agents were still *up*stairs. I started up, and when I looked up the stairs, I saw Susan's hand."

Nan Newby hoped the detective would leave her alone. New to real-estate, she could not believe what was happening on her first house tour, but she had to say it: "Meryl, I don't remember your carrying a folder. I remember only your purple purse."

Meryl clutched her purse tightly and hoped she wouldn't be asked to open her carry-all purse to show the contents. She wilted Nan with a glance.

Under Detective McRae's questioning stare, Nan felt she had to add something more. "I just followed Meryl and Tipper through the house. As I'm a new sales agent, I wanted to hear their comments. We had agreed to stay together, but in our enthusiasm for the place, we wandered in different directions. That's when I happened upon Susan sitting at her dressing table. She appeared relaxed and happy to see me. So I told her I was disappointed in not getting the listing. She shouted at me . . . I hadn't expected that. Terribly embarrassed, I spun on my heels and left." Nan nattered on nervously. "About five minutes later, Meryl and I met up again, but she said she wanted to retrace her steps to find a folder that she had left somewhere. After that was when I heard something banging around, and I heard a kitty meowing. But it's such a huge place, who knew where those noises came from . . . a huge place . . . it needs a large family. Then somehow, I managed to find the kitchen, and saw that Glen had beat us there. I had heard about this interesting glass bar, and I was eager to see it."

"We waited here for Meryl, wondering where she was," Tipper said. "Then we heard the sirens, but we couldn't tell where they were headed. And after the sirens settled down, Merle came in to join us and told us the ghastly news."

The Tyson Realty salespeople fidgeted. It was getting on to lunchtime, and they each hoped Detective McRae would wrap this up, so they could leave. They sat at the long glass bar restlessly swiveling on the stools. The detective knew they were anxious to leave, but he was not ready to let them go.

"Does Ms King have a cat? Does anyone know?" McRae asked.

No one answered. Glen knew, of course, but the less information he gave away about himself, the better—at least at this time.

"If so, perhaps there's a litter-box somewhere in the house; perhaps in an upper bathroom," McRae said. "I keep hearing a cat."

"Oh, yes, there's a litter-box in the dressing alcove off the master bedroom. It's on the back of the house overlooking the formal garden." As soon as she had spoken, Meryl wished she hadn't.

Detective McRae looked through the glass bar at Meryl's legs dangling from the stool, and saw her purple platform shoes. For a minute, he studied their deep purple pattern. Strange shoes, he thought. While the agents continued to squirm, McRae recorded impressions in his notebook, and then he dismissed them, saying he would have more questions later. He wanted to study the house layout, talk to the crime scene technicians before they left, and learn whether a likely murder weapon had been found.

On his way, he pulled out his mobile phone and punched a key to speed dial Johanna's number. He wanted to tell her that he was on a case, but would have no problem getting home in time to cook. Her message kicked in. He would try again later. He had nothing new to say—they had already agreed to meet at his house at 6:30 for dinner.

He took the staircase leading up from the kitchen. He pulled gloves from his pocket, put them on, and started down a long hallway, opening doors as he went. He could hear the commotion still coming from the crime scene. Soon, he found what he was looking for: a kitty. Shut in a linen closet. "What on earth! Who shut you in here, little guy?" Little guy only mewed—grateful to be free. "You'd better come along with me. No one will be here to give you kibbles."

He remembered that Meryl Tyson had been the only person who admitted seeing the litter-box, and he wanted to find it; see where Ms Tyson was at that time. With the kitty tucked under his arm, he headed toward the commotion at the back of the house. There he found the crime-crew captain, Officer Mary Knowles, and discussed with her the futility of finding significant fingerprints, as the sales agents had probably handled every banister and doorknob. They would have to hope that the instrument used to bludgeon Susan King would have prints other than hers. Then he asked Officer Knowles about the litter-box and, yes, it was in the alcove attached to the master bedroom. It had been used recently.

"We knew you were eccentric, Andy," Mary Knowles said, "but since when did you start traveling with a cat?"

"Oh . . . he's training to be a crime crew-captain," McRae shot back. "I *think* he's a he. Some days you just can't tell."

The day was shaping up such that he could easily cook dinner for Johanna as planned. That familiar warm feeling came up. How nice to look forward to another evening with her. He had met her when he worked on a previous investigation. She had been widowed over a year—he had caught her at just the right time before that attractive woman connected with someone else. And she and he were getting on nicely. He had already laid in the steaks and a fine wine. The grill was ready, but it was too chilly out for them to sit on the back patio. He thought about the wood fire that he was going to build. He would pour Johanna a glass of wine and leave her with Flicker before the fire, while he put on the steaks. He would make a salad first, of course. The meal was planned and she would arrive at 6:30. Clearly, Flicker liked Johanna as well. McRae wondered what Johanna and Flicker would think—about his bringing home the new little guy.

He dialed Johanna's number again. This time the message told him the account was full. Not taking messages.

The annoying image that wouldn't leave Meryl Tyson alone was Susan King's body after it hit the floor. *She did not lie over by the staircase.* Meryl was sure of it. She recalled that she had stared at the still body, dazed at what she had done, then ran from the room and went down the first hall and staircase that she could find. She had wanted to get away from the body. It was then she remembered that she had become terrified of being alone in that monster of a house with ghosts who may have seen what she did to Susan. Meryl had rushed along, going in circles through unfamiliar hallways, until she thought she heard Tipper and Nan upstairs. She found another staircase and started up. But before she had taken four steps she looked up and saw the bloody hand.

That bitch! Meryl didn't know which one she wanted to kill, Glen or Susan, but Susan had been handy. *Of course, Glen knew Susan well.* Meryl finally knew that. His picture stood large and crystal-framed by Susan's bed. And that blasted cat that did not want to leave the body alone. Had to shut the thing up. If she had known where the laundry chute was, that cat would have been laundry. She knew she must not touch anything. At least she couldn't leave prints on the cat; that was a mercy. But the picture frame with which she had slugged Susan—well, she had hastily tried to wipe it.

Better to hide it in her purse. Thank goodness she had brought the large purple Coach bag.

On his way home Detective McRae once more dialed Johanna's line and heard the message that the account was full. He was a bit puzzled but not worried; he knew her well enough to know she was reliable.

He arrived home about 5:00 p.m.—plenty of time to arrange for Flicker and little guy to meet. His plan was to shut the little kitty—he'd have to come up with a name—in a room by himself (was it a *he*?) until he was assured that the cats would get along. But right away Flicker started purring and grooming the new kitty. No problem in that area.

After a quick shower, Andy changed to his off-duty uniform of a sweater and khaki pants. Then he arranged wood in the fireplace and started a fire. Next, he made sure there was ice in case Johanna wanted a cold drink. He set the table, and checked the grill. He tried her phone again. No answer. At 7:00 he decided to drive by her house, to see if something was wrong.

He rang the doorbell and waited. No one came to the door. He stood there wondering what to do. Should he go around to the back? He couldn't see into the locked garage to know whether her car was in. He didn't want to be a snoop, but now he was concerned. Maybe, in the cause of friendship—and even more than friendship—he would be justified in looking in the windows. He looked in the front—all was in order. He went around the side and looked in—nothing amiss. But, when he got to the kitchen window in back, he dialed 911. Johanna was lying on the floor.

He came in late from the hospital. Johanna had been standing on a chair to reach something, had lost her balance, fallen backward, and cracked a cervical vertebra. She would be okay the doctor assured him. She could move all her parts; thank goodness, he thought. Now, when she was released from the hospital, he would get to cook for her more often; in the midst of trouble, there is always a good side—he enjoyed cooking and especially he enjoyed having a special person to cook for.

The cats, curled up together, ignored McRae when he came in. Despite the problems, he had a feeling of peace; things were as good as they could be, considering. Their steaks would keep, and tonight he would have a bowl of chili with cheddar melted over the top. Tomorrow he had to work on the Susan King crime. And, most important, find time to visit Johanna in the hospital again, and take her a tempting dinner.

In the morning he showered, dressed, and started a pot of coffee. He fed the cats, changed their water, and checked the litter-box to be sure that new kitty had found it. No problem there either. Little guy needed a name. He dialed Johanna's cell phone at the hospital.

"Good morning, Johanna, I have a serious problem."

"Oh, no . . . haven't we enough problems," she said.

"This is a *serious* one, though. I need a good name for a new kitty."

"That's just the kind of problem I need right now," she laughed.

"I thought that would keep you busy. Give you something to think about," he said. It felt so good to hear her laughter.

"Is it a girl, or a boy?" Johanna asked.

"Heck. I don't know. I'll make that your mission . . . to find out. Give you a reason to heal fast and get home. All I can tell you is that, male or female . . . Flicker likes it."

McRae told Johanna how he had wound up with another cat. Johanna told McRae that she ought to be out of the hospital in two, possibly three, days. After he hung up, he poured a cup of coffee and sat at the kitchen table to spread before him the notes and photos he had printed from his mobile. Back to work, he thought; let's think this through. The Tyson Realty employees had been fingerprinted, although McRae didn't know what help that would be, but certainly must be of some help—if the murder weapon turned up. He expected to hear from the medical examiner whether DNA had been collected under Susan King's fingernails. Something pecked at the back of McRae's brain; that *evidence bird* that bothered him sometimes. Something he was missing. Something he had noticed but could not recall.

He asked Flicker what he thought, but Flicker simply flicked his tail indecisively.

"Huh!" McRae grunted. "You'd better watch out or you'll be off the payroll."

He stood up, stretched, refreshed his coffee, and did a couple deep knee bends to keep the circulation flowing. He sat down again and rearranged his notes. Any of the agents could have been alone with the victim at the time of the attack. *Someone* was. Meryl Tyson had revealed this by knowledge of the litter-box location. Nan had been heard having a shouting match with the victim. And Glen—what about Glen? He seemed to have known about a cat in the mansion. Where did that knowledge come from? And Glen's eyes had been red; he seemed to be suffering over something. And, there was something puzzling about his not walking through the house with the other brokers. After all, it was his listing. Glen was hiding something. They were all hiding something. Even Tipper had been left alone upstairs. Did she have a reason to smash Ms King? None that McRae knew so far. But someone struck Susan King, and with what?

And why was she in the house when she had said she would be out? Telephone records might reveal a clue and his associate, Detective Chuck Nelson, was working on that now. However, McRae had to assume that there would be many calls regarding the listing. He had advised each of the realtors to stay in town; he would have further questions.

When men's clothing turned up in Susan King's huge walk-in closet—in particular, a navy-blue Tyson Realty blazer with the bright gold Tyson Realty emblem, and when many phone calls were recorded from Glen Chapman to Ms King, Detective McRae called Glen in for further questions.

"Yes, Detective, Susan and I were close. I didn't want it known because Meryl Tyson is the highly sensitive, jealous type . . . if you catch my meaning. Susan let me use a room upstairs for my office, and when I heard sirens pulling up to the house, not knowing what had happened, I hurriedly covered up any evidence that I was using an office at the manor, then I beat it down to the kitchen. Soon I learned from the others that something had happened to Susan. She had planned to go shopping, and I, sadly, had thought she was probably already out of the house. Sorry to say that I have been misguided by my association with Meryl."

Detective McRae could see that Glen was suffering.

"I didn't need to preview the house. I know it pretty well. So what was on my mind was beating the others to the kitchen so they wouldn't see me working in my office. I had no reason to hurt Susan . . . I loved her. I was looking forward to moving with her, but until I could find another realty position, I didn't want it to get out beforehand and hurt my commissions with Tyson Realty. Meryl thinks she owns me. Heart and soul . . . . And body.

"Then you knew a kitty was living there."

"Yes, sir."

"Do you want the kitty?"

"No. Right now my life is too uncertain and unsettled to think clearly about what's next."

Later, McRae thought that he should have asked Glen what gender the kitty was, and what its name was. Life's big missed opportunities, he laughed to himself.

Next, Detective McRae wanted to talk to Nan. Was Nan guilty? Telephone records showed that Nan had phoned Susan three times, and not from the office, but from her condominium at around dinnertime. Why had she not mentioned that?

When he and Detective Nelson stopped by Nan's condominium, she invited them in. Her living room was orderly but extremely modest and McRae could see why she would have appreciated being the broker to list Goldbrick Mansion. In that case no matter which broker actually found a buyer, Nan would have earned ten-percent of the sale. Not chump change.

"I thought being a new sales agent, inexperienced and all, that my chance for Susan to list with me was slim," Nan said. "If she would, I wanted to surprise the office. If she wouldn't, no one would be the wiser that I was brave enough to ask. I called Susan several times because she kept leading me on. At first she acted as if she would give me the listing, and later, I confronted her with her deception. That's when Meryl heard the yelling. But why would I have wanted to hurt Susan? She said she would let me be the one to show her something to buy after the mansion sold. She wanted to move to a smaller, more reasonably sized house."

Technicians had found no fingerprints that could significantly implicate anyone. As expected, Tyson Realty agents' prints matched those found on many stair railings and door handles. A struggle did not appear to have occurred: no DNA under fingernails, no attack instrument found, no fabric threads, or hairs found, no scratches, nothing that could help the investigation.

Equal weight could be placed on the guilt of Meryl Tyson, as well as on Tipper Thorp and Nan Newby: Meryl, because she had admitted seeing the litter-box near the hallway where Susan's body was found; Nan, because she had been disappointed in not obtaining the listing, and had owned up to a shouting match with Susan; and Tipper, just because she had been alone upstairs. Although at some point they had *all* been alone upstairs. Even Glen could have been the last to see Susan alive. He knew the mansion so well—he could have dealt the fatal blow and have gotten out quickly. Who knows what tensions existed between Glen and Susan? She could have found out that he and Meryl Tyson had something going on that had nothing to do with real-estate. Detective McRae would not stop searching for the weapon. That should tell a lot.

"Ms Tyson, I thought I would ask you to show me a house," Detective McRae said. "My significant other and I are talking about joining our lives, and neither of our homes is large enough for two adults, and two cats." McRae sat in the Tyson Realty office facing Meryl across her front desk. Susan King's fatality was three days in the past, and he was still on the trail.

Meryl was cheerful. Things were going well. Tyson Realty still had the listing for

Goldbrick Mansion, and Glen, although he acted distracted, was around the office more.

"Let me get you a cup of coffee and I'll show you videos of some good choices."

When Meryl stepped out back for coffee, McRae stood and stretched. He could see down a narrow aisle between the agents' offices. At the rear of the aisle was a window through which he saw a large green dumpster. That gave him an idea.

"I'm sorry, Ms Tyson," he called to her, "but, uh . . . I just remembered something for which I have to hurry."

As soon as he closed the Tyson Realty door, he called Detective Nelson to have that dumpster searched. Immediately. If he were lucky, it had not been emptied since the murder. "Also, ask the judge for a warrant for a pair of purple shoes which will be found at Meryl Tyson's home. I hope."

While he waited for the dumpster search, he went home and started a beef stew. He wouldn't have time to get it cooked tonight for Johanna, who was still in the hospital, but it would be perfect for tomorrow night. He had just talked to her and had said he would be visiting her in a few hours after he simmered the stew and fed the cats. Johanna sounded happy about that.

At about 8:00 p.m., he was walking down the hospital corridor with Johanna on his arm, when Detective Nelson phoned from headquarters.

"We may have found the weapon, Andy. Get ready for this . . . it's a heavy, ten-by-twelve, crystal picture frame, containing a man's photo and possibly blood smears. We're sending it for DNA and prints."

"Hold it . . . I'll be right down," McRae said. "I want to see it first."

"Ms Tyson," McRae said. "I'm surprised at you . . . with your years of experience and business acumen, that you would carelessly throw the photo of Glen in your dumpster." Meryl Tyson had just opened her front door to find Detectives McRae and Nelson. This business never seems to end, she thought; she had hoped it was all over.

"That doesn't mean I had anything to do with Susan King's death."

"Well . . . Ms Tyson," McRae drawled it out, "the photo is signed by Glen Chapman, and the writing on the photo says, 'To Susan with great love.' Moreover, Glen Chapman says he gave it to Susan. You need a good reason why your fingerprints were found on the frame, along with Susan's DNA, and . . . the frame was found in your office's dumpster. Oh, it's clear that someone attempted to erase the prints, but didn't manage. Also, I have a warrant to pick up your purple platform shoes. I am interested in the dark spots I remember seeing on them. I believe, even though you have probably cleaned the shoes by now, that the lab will find Susan's DNA on them."

McRae quoted the Miranda warning to her, and Nelson stepped forward with handcuffs.

Meryl was speechless. For a while it had appeared that she had gained everything. But, she had really lost everything.

"The new kitty is a female. A little girl," Johanna said. She was sitting before Andy McRae's fire with a glass of Clos Lambrays dry Burgundy, 2004. "Couldn't you tell?"

"I'm a people detective," he said. "Not a cat detective."

"You found him . . . or rather, her . . . didn't that take a bit of feline detection?"

"Quite a bit, considering the size of that mansion. But I don't think the department will give me a commendation for that."

"That's inconsiderate. I'll have to file a formal complaint."

Johanna had been released from the hospital and it was celebration time. McRae had picked her up and had brought her to his house for a cozy dinner before the wood fire. He had solved the Susan King case. Meryl Tyson had confessed that her emotions got out of control, and in a fit of jealous rage over seeing Glen's picture on Susan's bureau; she had snatched it, and with it slugged Susan. She was horrified that she had killed her and actually, for a time, hadn't remembered doing so.

"Johanna, congratulations for your speedy recovery; I drink a toast to that." Andy raised his glass. "And if you ever stand on another ladder, two cats and I want to be there holding on to you and the ladder. The cats will hold on to the ladder, and, if you don't mind, I will hold on to you."

"But I didn't stand on a ladder . . . I stood on a chair," she glinted at him mischievously.

"Whatever!"

"And I drink a toast to your case being solved. Sharp thinking."

"Well, actually," Andy said, "I had clear clues. Kitty even helped. Meryl Tyson said she had seen a litter-box. Had she not been in the alcove off Ms King's master bedroom, she would not have seen that box. It's true that a broker would look everywhere, but it was the coincidence of finding the body close by, that set me thinking. And Meryl Tyson's outrageous purple platform shoes! That was another clue that I missed at first. When I sat across from Ms Tyson at that monstrous glass bar, and looked through the glass at those shoes, you might say they spoke to me; at that time just not loudly enough. Something about those shoes . . . they did not look right, and for good reason . . . they were splattered with Susan King's blood in a manner, that if one didn't look closely, could just have been a pattern on the fabric. Well, that's enough shop talk for now," Andy said. "I'm going out to put our steaks on the grill. You stay here and keep warm by the fire. It's raw out."

"Before you go," Johanna said. "I have a good name for kitty: 'Agatha.' She helped to solve the crime."

Andy thought about that. "How about 'Christi'? It goes down better. Let's ask the cats. They vote, you know . . . and it's two guys against two gals."

"Ummm, I don't think we'll get far with that."

Death Deals a Blow
at Spangle Dangle Specialties

When Ron Simmons, the manager of Spangle Dangle Specialties, came in the back door to the store and saw his employee, Emma Copley, lying bloody and lifeless, he called the police immediately. Detective Mark Greeley had arrived shortly after the police.

"It's horrible," Ron said to Detective Greeley. "This is how I found her. There's no evidence of a break-in, but someone had to have deactivated the security system." They looked around at ceramic tiles, broken and scattered about the body. "And where did this box of tiles come from? Could it have been placed on that shelf over the door, and struck her when she came in? Most extraordinary!"

Detective Greeley lived nearby and had rushed out after quickly pulling on jeans and the Hawaiian shirt he had thrown over the bedside chair hours earlier. He had arrived just as the police were taping off the rear parking lot, and crime scene techs were unloading their van. While he watched the technicians photograph and mark off the area around the body, he listened to Ron's conversation with the police. He saw that Emma Copley's head was bashed in and bloody. He noted the broken tiles that lay smashed across the room. Hands in pockets, he paced around, staying out of the way.

Julie Hansen, the bookkeeper, brushed hair off her brow and tried to compose herself. Her eyes teared as she attempted to tell Detective Greeley what had happened.

"Emma called me this morning at about 6:45 to ask whether she could borrow my keys. She hadn't noticed until she was ready to leave for work that her Spangle keys had gone missing." Julie paused for a minute before she could go on. "So . . . about fifteen minutes later she came by and I gave her my key. Emma was an inventory clerk and had worked here for several years. We trusted her completely." Julie tried to suppress a sob so that she could continue to be helpful.

"Did she have any idea where she had lost her keys?"

"She didn't say. She was hurried trying to beat the delivery guy . . . he usually arrives first thing. Emma was unusually quiet, though. Maybe that was what she was trying to solve."

Boxes of merchandise to be put away, some for the expansive show room and some for the back storeroom, were stacked inside the rear entrance. Next to the door, a twelve-foot stepladder leaned up against the back wall. Behind Detective Greeley was an open door into the storeroom where inventory waited until it could be moved to the showroom. Greeley turned into this room and looked around. Filling the room, side-by-side and reaching the ceiling, were long racks of merchandise destined for display. Some items were of delicate and fragile china or pottery. Others were of less-destructible wood and leather. He looked for any clue that might point to the crime. Finding nothing remarkable, he returned to the lifeless body.

"Who is usually the first to arrive and open up?" Greeley asked Ron.

"Except for Mondays and Thursdays, when early shipments arrive, I'm always the first in," Ron said. "During the busy season as manager I have more work than I can sometimes keep up with and have to put in more hours. But I knew that today, Emma planned to get here early for the delivery." Ron tried to gather his thoughts, his eyes avoided Emma's body. "This is so hard to believe . . . a lovely gal . . . she was such a good employee, a sweetheart. And hard working." He brushed away tears.

Detective Greeley listened, took notes, and watched forensic techs gathering evidence. They dusted for fingerprints, as well as employed an argon-ion laser. Greeley watched as the techs paid careful attention to the aluminum ladder, dusting it with a black powder, looking for any piece of evidence. He saw them carefully remove and put into an evidence bag, a scrap of fabric that was stuck in a hinge on the ladder. He thought he had examined the ladder during the night. How did he miss that scrap? He quickly tucked in his shirt. Let anyone who notice think he had rushed to dress. Which was true, actually.

"Did Ms Copley talk about any fears she had? Anyone threatening her?" Greeley asked Ron.

"No. Not to me. Maybe Adam knows something about that. Emma was dating Adam Walker, my other inventory clerk. He's off today. They were planning to live together." Ron paused and swallowed hard, words tight in his throat. "She told me she looked forward to helping Adam finish school. He works here to help pay for college, and has another year to go for his degree." For a moment Ron couldn't continue; the pain of thinking forward to when Adam would receive this terrible news. "I can't bear to tell him."

A sneer plied the detective's features and he interrupted, "So, who all have keys to the store?"

Ron attempted to think and to give the detective straight answers. "Julie Hansen, Emma Copley, Adam Walker, and I, of course, are the only ones with keys. We park in back and come in the back door. The sales associates park out front. As you can see, the narrow back alley has only limited parking and is used for loading and unloading. We let both Emma and Adam park in the rear since they often arrive early to receive shipments . . . or we did," he said sadly. He paused again before he could go on.

"Actually, one of us always gets here a bit early to let sales associates in the front door when they ring the bell." He kicked a piece of tile and sent it sliding across the room. "Emma told me she really enjoyed coming in here each day. She said the candle aromas were uplifting. They had a reviving impact on her during late nights keeping Adam company while he clocked homework." Ron's face was pinched with grief.

Julie cut in and rambled on nervously trying to make sense of this tragedy. "Adam and

Emma were so happy to have found each other. Someone will have to reach Adam at his apartment and tell him this horrible news. He'll be crushed . . . like the rest of us."

The front door bell rang. Ron walked through the store to open the door and herd the arriving sales associates into the employee lounge. "Wait here," he said to them, "I'll explain shortly."

The sales people punched their cards into the time clock, took aprons from a hook, and took a seat. They had seen the police cars, and in hushed tones, murmured their astonishment to each other.

As Detective Greeley stood nearby and observed, Police Captain Chuck McEwan turned to him and said: "An unpleasant sight we have here. An innocent woman taken down for no apparent reason."

He's assuming a lot, Greeley thought, but he hiked his brow, nodded, and said nothing. He wondered whether McEwan had heard about his peace-disturbing incident. Probably not—he had thrown that fit several towns away. That night was just an irritating memory that scratched the inside of his brain. Things had gone a little sideways then. What did that little shit, Emma, take him for? He wasn't naïve or something. That story that she just needed a month or so to get her head together—she couldn't treat him like that. He wasn't stupid; there must be someone else, he had thought at the time. They had dated two months and he expected that Emma was his, and only his. Women! He had raged until the restaurant called the police, and called a taxi to take Emma home. Okay! Okay, he had said. He hadn't been drinking. He hadn't thrown anything or hit anyone, so the police let him go. The restaurant did not press charges.

Detective Greeley and Captain McEwan sat in the office to recap what they had learned so far. Only four people had keys, said McEwan: "Ron Simons, the manager, who was the first to arrive and who found the body; Julie Hansen, the bookkeeper, who loaned Emma keys; and the two inventory clerks: Emma Copley, the victim, and Adam Walker, who has today off. The alarm wasn't triggered, and there's no sign of forced entry. It looks as though when she stepped in, she got dumped on from the shelf above the door. One fatal blow. Clearly something attached to the inner doorknob was anchored somehow to the box of tiles on that shelf. The box has creases where something was tied around it."

"Yeah . . . I noticed that," Detective Greeley said.

"Then, when she opened the door," the captain repeated his logic, "and stepped in, something yanked down the box, dealing a blow to her skull. A nasty way to go."

Greeley nodded his head.

"I've asked the staff, and no one remembers whether the box of tiles was on the shelf before today, but they doubt it," McEwan said. "Something that heavy is normally stored in the back storage room." A few seconds of quiet held the room while McEwan thought that through.

Greeley was quiet. Atypically quiet.

"How about an early lunch, Gree? My treat. I think I owe you from last year, don't I? I'm going to wrap up here and turn in my report. We can meet at Bertucci's."

"Sounds like a plan," Greeley said. "Spangle will have to open soon; they've already delayed opening. I heard Julie and Ron talking about keeping the store closed for the day. But they concluded that keeping busy would be the best balm for dealing with this, and for keeping it quiet, at least for a bit."

Though his shirt was already tucked in, he gave it another tuck as he turned to see the front entrance. "There's a crowd waiting to get in. I noticed that a tech went around to photograph them; see if we can catch the perp returning to the crime scene. When they open, the sales people will be busy. I'll talk to them after lunch."

"I'm eager to hear what you find," McEwan said. "How did he . . . or she . . . get in? That person had to have had a key. They may have used that ladder to stage the tiles over the door, and in the process, caught a piece of clothing in the ladder's hinge. That may be an important clue. We'll be interested in seeing what prints were left, but that probably won't be much help since employees' prints will be all over, including the ladder."

Greeley nodded. The less said the better.

When Detective Greeley arrived at Bertucci's, he spotted Captain McEwan waving his hand to signal him over. He joined him at his table.

"Ah . . . I see you changed clothes," McEwan said.

"Yeah . . . after I got out of there, the stink from all those hundreds of candles stuck to my clothing, and I smelled too 'purdy.' I couldn't stand it. So I made a quick change. I don't live far from here, just down by the river." He nervously adjusted items on the table, moving the salt and pepper to a different spot, sliding the menu card a few inches.

McEwan watched this action.

"But, before I left Spangle," Greeley said, "I asked the sales people whether they had seen anything unusual . . . they don't know anything."

The detective was bored with it all, bored with this case, more interested in the menu. He suggested they order a shrimp cocktail and a Margarita pizza. But he would forgo beer since he would be going back to Spangle for interrogations.

"Earlier I saw you talking to the bookkeeper, Julie," Greeley said. "Did she have anything helpful to add?"

"Julie said Emma had been thrilled about dating Adam Walker and about the plans they were making. She said that Emma and Adam had met each other at Spangle, and she was proud about that."

The waiter set the shrimp before them and for a few minutes, they paid attention to their stomachs.

"'Spang Dang.' That's what they call it," said Greeley, thinking out loud. But he wished he hadn't said that. He spiked a shrimp and dispatched it to his mouth.

"Oh yeah . . . I hadn't heard that. Where'd you pick that up?"

"I don't know. Just around," Greeley said, his mouth working the shrimp.

"Sounds like a company in China."

"Well, yeah. Probably most of the stuff is made in China."

As they ate, Captain McEwan tried to pull out more of the detective's thoughts. Greeley had a reputation for keen insight into crimes.

But Greeley was rather quiet; his attention full on the pizza which sat before them.

After they had finished eating, McEwan said, "I've must get back to the office. I'll walk you to your car. Let me know when you finish interrogations and file your report. I trust we'll soon learn who got there before Emma."

As Detective Greeley ducked into his car, he saw McEwan staring at the clothes in the back seat.

"On your way to the dry cleaners, I see."

"Yeah. Crime doesn't stop the common chore."

He's entirely too nosy, Greeley thought, and, as he drove down Main Street, he turned into the driveway that led down to the library's rear parking lot. For a few minutes, he waited there to see whether McEwan had followed him. If so, he would park the car, go into the library and look for a book as though that were normal. If McEwan did not turn down to the parking lot, he would wait twenty minutes, then pull out onto the street and over to the dry cleaners. He remembered that a tailor worked there. She would be able to cut off the torn area and take a hem in his shirt. There was plenty of length in the shirt for that.

Back at the store, Detective Greeley asked the three sales associates to come to the employee lounge one at a time, where they could speak privately. He took a seat at a long table in the middle of the room and pushed aside unwashed cups, paper napkins, and plastic utensils that were strewn about. Along the walls were open boxes of samples and flyers, and on an opposite wall a sign that admonished: "Your mother doesn't work here. Clean up after yourself."

The first associate to come back was Scott Walker. Greeley asked him to take a seat. Scott dropped coins into a machine and took time selecting his choice. Finally, he punched down a coke and fingered out his change. Then he scraped a chair across the tiled floor and sat, leaning back, legs splayed—and stared at the detective. Although he was in shock about Emma, whom he had really liked, he would treat this like the break it was and try to relax. The detective waited for him to open the can.

"Scott, what can you tell me about Emma? This is looking like an intentional act. Was she in some kind of trouble, or did someone have a grudge against her?"

Scott took his time answering. "No. I feel sure of that. She was too easy-going to create animosity in anyone. She was always quick to help . . . to help us find in inventory a special customer request. And, she was stoked to be dating Adam." He drank from the can, then swirled it around on the table, making circles in the condensation.

Greeley waited.

"Before that, she was having trouble with some third-rail she was seeing."

"Tell me about that," Greeley said.

"Well, I don't know who he was. Seems she preferred to keep it to herself. But, a couple mornings her eyes were red. She didn't want to talk about it, and I respected her privacy. It's too bad now that I didn't find out more about it. She worked in the back and I worked in sales, so we rarely had time to gab."

Next, Greeley called Kimberly Smith back to the lounge. She brought bottled water with her and drank from it as she and the detective talked. She didn't seem nervous in the least, nor in a hurry. A cute gal, she was carefully made up, and Greeley could see below her apron her skinny jeans over skinny, but shapely, legs—exactly his kind of woman. And she smiled at him—even in the midst of this tragedy. In fact, she smiled sweetly at him. Special, he thought, and he jacked up his professional demeanor. He thought he knew the answer, but he wanted to ask it again.

"Which of the employees have keys?"

She gave him the four names and explained that Adam, who was out today, and Emma had keys because some deliveries arrive before or after the store is closed. They would open so the driver could off-load the shipment and be on his way. Kimberly didn't need to be prodded, she spilled over with information. "They don't have to do that, since deliveries are scheduled, but they know the hazard of driving up I-91, and how that could throw off a delivery. Among the four of them, one always arrives ahead of the rest of us, and lets us in when we ring the front bell. The front door is kept locked of course, until the store opens."

"So you can't get in unless one of them is here," Greeley said.

"Correct."

"Tell me whatever you know about Emma. Was she having problems with anyone? That box of tiles may have been pulled off on purpose. It's looking like someone was here before her."

"That's what's strange, for the accident must have happened around 8:00, an hour before opening. No one gets here that early except Adam, Emma, and sometimes, Ron. I can't imagine who else could have been here. And the rumor reaching us at the sales counter is that there was no sign of a break-in."

"Had you heard any names? Names of anyone she may have been dating? Names of anyone who may have wanted to hurt her?" Greeley couldn't say 'kill'.

"Well, the last two months, or so," Kimberly said, "Emma and Adam were dating. We were all happy for them. They got along splendidly, and had nothing but good to say about each other." She frowned as she paused to drink water.

"Go on," Greeley said. "Did she mention anyone else?"

"Emma was on the quiet side, and she worked in the back with inventory. So we didn't chat often, but she did confide to me that a guy she had dated for a couple months was threatening her. She said she told him she didn't want to see him again and he wouldn't accept it. Emma said he was demanding, and she was afraid he would become abusive. He had made a scene in a restaurant when she said she wouldn't be seeing him anymore. She said she told him she didn't like being controlled; that she was a grown woman, earning her way, and in charge of her life."

"Did she ever mention a name, or tell you anything about this guy?"

"No. And as far as I know, he never came to see her at the store. She was rather private, and besides, as I said, when on duty, we don't have much time for gossip."

The information that Amber Taylor, another sales associate, had to give, was about the same. Nothing new. She was sad for Adam, and knew what a loss this would be for him. He and Emma had seemed perfect for each other. And no, she had no idea who else might have been in Emma's life, or who might have wanted to hurt her.

Finally, Detective Greeley again questioned Ron, the manager, and Julie, the bookkeeper, but they could add nothing new.

"Where would tile normally be stored?" he asked Ron. "I'm sure, being so heavy, not over the door."

"I'll show you," Ron said and he walked the detective back to the storeroom and pointed out racks where boxes of tiles were stored. "Customers buy these tiles for tabletops, and we sell the tables for mix-and-match. But you can see that since the boxes are so heavy, they are placed on a bottom shelf. It does look as though a box was removed recently." He kneeled and pointed out a dust smear, then stood and looked around the racks. "Nothing else looks disturbed."

"What about the ladder by the back entry?" Greeley asked.

"That ladder always stays by that door for convenience. That's one of the few open spots where we can put it. It's used all over the store."

Detective Greeley, beer in hand, pushed back in the lounge chair. The balmy, late-spring evening was perfect for soothing his spirit. He watched the moon play notes over the river's gentle ripples. The lights of Rocky Brook flashed on the opposite shore. The location of his cottage near the ferry landing was perfect, he mused—it just needed a woman. Thinking back, Greeley recalled the point when he had known what he had to do. Emma couldn't belong to anyone else; his obsession ruled. He would stage an accident. It had to be at Spangle where numerous people would be suspected. He knew Emma went in early on Thursdays; about 8:00 a.m. No one else arrived until 9:00. He also knew that she alternated this chore with the other inventory clerk, Adam Walker, the one she was seeing. The little twerp. The twerp came in early on Mondays. "Twerp clerk. Twerp clerk," he repeated the words. He remembered how he had gone to 'Spang Dang' on a day when he knew Emma wouldn't be there, and he had casually strolled to the back. He made it appear as though he thought it was another showroom. He had seen the ladder and the shelf over the rear entrance, and that had set him to thinking. The problem would be in getting a key, and then once inside quickly turning off the security system. A quick glance showed the system to be a kind he had deactivated many times.

After thinking about it some more, he had realized that getting Emma's key would be a cinch. He knew that she always placed her keys on a console just inside the front door of her apartment. The Spangle key hung on a cord with her I.D badge. If on a Wednesday night he could catch her at home, he would ring her bell, and when she came to the door, he would hand her flowers and say he had been thinking about her, but wouldn't come in. Then he would immediately press the button on a mobile phone in his pocket, causing Emma's pre-programmed number to ring. When she was distracted, both to answer her phone and to put the flowers in water, he would quickly step in and snitch her keys. With his years of practicing subterfuge, he could easily do that without her noticing. And so it had worked that way. He had even bought a throwaway mobile phone for that purpose.

The next day had been Thursday, and so that no one would see his car, he walked over—it was only a mile. He didn't worry about how she would get in without her key; he knew she would work that out. He recalled how he had let himself in to Spang in the middle of the night, and had arranged over the door something ready to push off when she came in. Something heavy from inventory that would fit on that shelf over the door and give her a good blow from above. What if someone else walked in first, he had wondered. Well, that was just a chance he had had to take. With any plan, no matter how perfect, there would always be a few ifs, ands, or buts.

He prided himself on that plan, and how well it had worked. He would think about it no more this night, but would go to bed soon and try not to dream about it. It was done and no one was the wiser. He would not have to share Emma with anyone, let alone Twerp Clerk.

The next day he finished his reports and submitted them to homicide. He had had to question the distraught twerp, Adam Walker, which put him in a foul mood—just seeing the twerp for whom Emma had left him. The twerp's roommate vouched that the twerp had not left the apartment the night of the crime. Greeley was pleased that interview was over, hurting as it was. The good news was that when Emma told the twerp that she had broken off with someone who had been a problem, she had been discrete; had mentioned no names; had gone into no detail.

Through for the day, Greeley tried to forget everything; blank out his mind as he sat relaxing on the patio. He watched the Connecticut River's fast-moving current as it captured flickers of the lowering sun, and once more deserted the village of Glastonbury. Despite his inner turmoil, the surrounding green trees and the quiet calmed him. He breathed in the cool and fragrant spring breezes. On his side of the river: beautiful, calm, open Glastonbury. The other side: aggressive, squeezed Rocky Brook. He could see the small ferry plowing across the river toward Rocky Brook. He had read that it was the oldest, continuously operating ferry in the U.S. Watching it made him feel like a part of its history.

It was cooler now, and he decided to go in. When he had just shut the door he heard a car turn into his driveway. He listened, his apprehension on alert. When the knock came, he waited five seconds, then opened the door.

"Hello, Gree, do you have a minute to talk? I have something to pass by you about the Emma Copley case," Captain McEwan said.

"Of course. Join me for a beer out on the patio?"

"Don't mind if I do."

Greeley directed McEwan to the patio, and on the way through the kitchen, stopped to get a beer for him. McEwan relaxed back in a lounge chair and watched the mesmerizing ripples flicker over the water. Though the sun was nearly down, there were enough lights along the river to reflect off gentle waves dancing along.

"What a wonderful spot," McEwan said. "A perfect view of the river. With its deep muddy bottom, it's the perfect place to dispose of crime evidence. Accessible from many spots in town, that river is probably where Emma's keys are. You know they've never turned up." McEwan worked on the beer, licking his lips.

He did not seem eager to come to his reason for stopping by.

Greeley nodded.

"Also, there's the puzzle of an unidentifiable number that rang her phone the night before she was killed," McEwan said. "It traces back to a non-existent number."

"Probably a marketing call. They don't like to be traced, lest someone complain," Greeley said.

"I'm sorry to have to bring up something so touchy," McEwan said, "but there's some inner-office gossip that you were having trouble with a woman in your life."

"Oh, don't I wish. It would be nice to have a woman in my life with or without trouble. Look around and let me know if you find one here." Greeley swigged his beer and laughed. "No, there's no one. Hasn't been for the past year or so."

"Well, there's another point I must bring up. When I looked into your car last week, I saw a Hawaiian shirt intended for the cleaners. I'm sure there's no connection, but I think the swatch that caught on the ladder at Spangle Dangle may match that shirt. What did you do with that shirt, Gree?"

"It's hanging right here in the damn closet. I'll bring it out. That has to be a coincidence. It couldn't be that shirt. It's in perfect shape."

He brought the shirt out on a hanger.

McEwan was embarrassed to have to examine it, but he must. He fingered it all around. The shirt was perfect. There could be no connection between it and the scrap found on the ladder at Spangle.

Greeley disappeared into the house for two more ice-cold beers and chips. They nursed the beer and quietly watched the last trace of the sun's light sink below the trees on the opposite bank.

"Well, that's one that Cold Cases can work on for the next ten years," McEwan said. "Everyone has an alibi. No one was there. The box just rigged itself over the door. Emma's time had come."

Greeley nodded knowingly. "Yup."

He watched Captain McEwan back out of the driveway. Then he took the shirt inside. Before hanging it up he looked at its new hem. He satisfied himself that there had been plenty of room to cut off the portion with the tear, and re-hem.

By now it was evening, but still pleasant on the patio. He sat back in the lounge chair and looked forward to a decent lapse of time when he might visit 'Spang Dang' and chat with Kimberly Smith. Maybe ask her for lunch. Or maybe even dinner. She looked like a gal who deserved the best and wasn't he the best! Hell, the future had possibilities. As he planned out the future, he watched the river sliding along on its eternal journey. And he pictured all that mud with a mobile phone and keys resting deep within.

The Mysterious Death
of Lady Harrod

Detective Chief Inspector Larry Hughes noticed the corpse's suspiciously red face that even the funeral home makeup could not conceal. He and his assistant, Sergeant Simon Turner, learned that before her death Lady Harrod had been having headaches, chest pains, and nausea. And, her blood was found to have high levels of cyanide. An anonymous call had come into headquarters about the death of Dowager Lady Harrod, and DCI Hughes and Sergeant Turner had been put on the case. The funeral was today.

The darkening day did nothing to lift the DCI's mood. On his way to the funeral, he reviewed the disagreement he had had the week before with Alena, his fiancée. They had been at the point of buying a cottage together and, it turned out, they had different needs—different ideas. Mainly, Alena wanted a fenced lawn for her dog, Oscar. But the house she had found did not have room for an office for DCI Hughes—an absolute requirement—and an office could not be added on. Whereas, the house Hughes had found, that had the perfect office, had no fenced lawn for Oscar. Their budget restricted their choices. They had said hard words; each not hearing the other's viewpoint. There must be a solution, a compromise of some sort, he thought. He had called her several times during the week with no answer.

"Mr. Puddy, did you get sight of Miss Wright?" Mrs. Ward, head housekeeper for the recently deceased Lady Harrod, asked the butler. They had just returned from Lady Harrod's funeral. Lady Harrod's servants barely had time to gather behind the family to witness the casket being lowered into the dirt, before they had to return to the manor to organize the kitchen. Fifty or more family members and friends would soon come into the manor for high tea, and to continue their mourning. And socializing.

"Yes," Puddy said, "and she did not look well, although I could get only a side glimpse. I saw someone else of note who looked quite chipper . . . Miss Lydia Jones."

"No, Mr. Puddy! Surely not."

"I say I did, Mrs. Ward."

"Some nerve that one has. I'm surprised she didn't move up to the front row at the gravesite to try to sit by Lord Nigel."

Although the early December weather was drizzly and cold, Lady Harrod's funeral was heavily attended. Family, friends, and servants came, as well as DCI Hughes and Sergeant Turner, of the East Knoyliss police. The dowager had a fortune and a large estate to leave. Nearly everyone except the two detectives sobbed quietly, but out of the corners of the mourners' eyes, they watched each other. Each relative hoped to be treated handsomely in Lady Harrod's will. But there had been rumors of foul play with respect to the old gal.

A damp mist hung over the yellow fields. Women dabbed their eyes and hugged their coats against the chill. Men assured every one of their grief by frequently reaching for their handkerchiefs. From off to the side, behind the servants, DCI Hughes and Sergeant Turner watched. In particular, they noted sitting in front, Lady Harrod's two daughters—Lady Abigail Hawthorne, and her younger sister,

Lady Jane Stuart, with her son, Lord Nigel Stuart. DCI Hughes noticed that among all the mourners Lord Nigel grieved the most openly. When the final *Requiescat in Pace* was uttered, the group slowly passed the casket, some placing on it a pebble or scattered dirt, then walked from the family plot down Church Lane and into the manor. The two detectives mingled with the guests making their way into the grand hall.

The eighteen-meter table was heavily laden the length of it with meats, greens, fruits, and pastries. And footmen circulated with crystal glasses of sherry. Several attendants stood ready to help Puddy in case he saw anything amiss or missing from the table. Grief hung on the servants' stooped shoulders, but still they must serve.

As she selected morsels for her plate, Lady Hawthorne nodded toward the other end of the long table and said to her sister, "Don't look now, but would you believe who is here?". Lady Stuart leaned forward to see around the crowd and saw Lydia, the infamous Lydia Jones. Lady Stuart looked back to her sister and rolled her eyes to the ceiling.

"It's most unsuitable for her to have come," Lady Stuart said.

The daughters continued to fill their plates. Their mother's funeral had not abated their appetites.

After waiting a day to let the Harrod family soothe its emotions, DCI Hughes made appointments to interrogate all family members and servants, and to ask them not to leave town. However, he was told that Lord Nigel had left early that morning for college, and would not be back until the holiday started. He was seen driving off in Lady Harrod's favorite sports car, with a woman at his side who looked like Miss Lydia Jones.

It was clear to DCI Hughes that the servants were the most distressed by Lady Harrod's demise. They had served her for many years and she had treated them with kindness and consideration, worrying about their health and families, and always remembering their special occasions. And because Lady Hawthorne and Lady Stuart no longer lived at the manor, Hughes and Turner met first with Puddy. Puddy invited them to sit in his own sitting room where a roaring fire would help lift his spirits. DCI Hughes asked most of the questions, and Sergeant Turner took notes as Puddy explained the position and status of family members, and servants. Hughes respected that, although Puddy was heart-broken by Lady Harrod's death, he would not easily indulge in gossip—even if he suspected foul play. Thus he would need careful persuasion.

"Lady Harrod's illness took a stronger grip each week, and about four days ago she fell into a coma," Puddy said. "Nothing could revive her. When milady first fell ill, her daughters had called in the best physicians from London: Doctor Quell and Doctor Treemor, and they came down immediately; Lady Harrod did not believe in going to hospitals. She thought, illogically, that more people died in hospital than at home."

DCI Hughes had to suppress a smile.

Puddy rang for a maid to serve tea and cakes.

"Did Lady Harrod get along well with her daughters and grandson, young Lord Nigel?" DCI Hughes asked.

"I don't consider it really of note, but allow me to say, sir, that . . . the relationship between Lady Harrod and her youngest daughter, Lady Stuart, was a bit strained."

"And how was that, Mr. Puddy?"

"Lady Harrod was too kind, sir, if I may say so. She denied nothing to Lady Stuart and the more she gave, the more was expected. When Lady Harrod began to say *no*, Lady Stuart turned a cold heart, sir, and stayed away. Lady Harrod would hear gossip about Lady Stuart. It broke her heart, sir."

"Indeed," DCI Hughes said. "And what was Lady Harrod's relationship with Load Nigel?"

"Well, sir, Lady Harrod doted on young Lord Nigel. Since his mother's divorce, and her subsequent falling out with Lady Harrod, his home has been here. But except for vacations, he was up at college. He comes down summers and holidays." Puddy tugged at his collar. Attempting to fill a quiet interval, he offered the men more tea.

Sergeant Turner, actively taking notes in a small notebook, flipped a page and continued writing.

"What did he do summers?" DCI Hughes urged on Puddy.

"When he wasn't off somewhere . . . who knows where . . . he worked with Lady Harrod in the gardens and orchards. We have gardeners of course, but the gardens were Lady Harrod's passion and she took pleasure working in them. Some seasons we saw her more on her knees in various gardens, than on her feet in the house. Lord Nigel worked alongside her when he was home. Together they would shovel, haul, and spread bone meal and potash all about. I observed that they would cover a layer of bone meal with a thin layer of potash. They said that discourages animals from digging. I believe, sir, the activity kept Lady Harrod's mind off the Lady Stuart problem."

"Indeed. That would be a good distraction," said DCI Hughes.

Encouraged by DCI Hughes's comment, Puddy resumed: "On hot days, I would take iced drinks out to them to assure they did not go thirsty. But even on gray, misty days, I would often find them there in gardening garb, raking and shoveling. Sometimes when Lord Nigel was home, and Lady Harrod was attending her Mothers' Club meeting, he worked in the gardens alone. Or, I would find him in the greenhouse."

"What is in the greenhouse, Mr. Puddy?"

"That's where certain ornamental plants and gardening tools, aprons, and shoes are kept. They were considerate not to track into the manor." Puddy paused to consider what else he could add. "Lord Nigel makes most of the compost. He does make a noise out there, grinding and grinding. We can hear it all the way to the manor. I understand that is part of his school effort—horticulture or chemistry."

Puddy sat still, his gaze far away wandering in memory. The men waited patiently.

"Every year Lady Harrod was asked to open the Upper Knoyless Fair," Puddy continued proudly. "A big event here, as you might imagine. And her produce and blossoms were among the best. Award winning." His throat tightened. "So sad, sir, to see her grow weaker and not up to tending her flowers."

"Right," said DCI Hughes. He paused for a respectable minute then asked, "So Lord Nigel is a responsible lad?"

Puddy squinted up his face and for a moment looked at the view outside the window, gray and damp. He yearned to turn it to sun, and back to the past. Then he pulled his gaze back into the room and said, "Well, sir, he is a bit on the untamed side. And, if you don't mind my saying so, he sometimes thinks he's the dog's bollocks."

"And Lady Harrod didn't mind that?"

"Young Nigel had a way with my mistress. For her, his smile stretched a mile, and his eyes had a special glint. And, I must add that he was always polite to the servants. But he was spoiled, sir, and he would go off on a bender with a young woman, Miss Lydia Jones, about whom, I'm afraid much gossip trails."

"How did Lady Harrod handle that?" Hughes asked.

"Lady Harrod didn't seem to notice. Or she didn't let on. But I know, sir, that one time in the past they argued when Lady Harrod said she would disinherit Lord Nigel if he did the unspeakable and married Miss Jones. After that we spotted him sneaking Miss Jones in the back way."

Puddy thought he saw a shadow move under the library door. DCI Hughes followed his gaze. Puddy lowered his voice. "I believe, sir, Lady Harrod may have wanted to make up for her problems with her daughter, Lady Stuart, Lord Nigel's mother, by being close to the young man. And he did win her over. Milady did not have much family left." Puddy changed the subject, happy to escape the hot seat. "I believe Lady Abigail Hawthorne has arrived. Would you care to speak with her now, sir?"

"Yes, Mr. Puddy, I have no more questions for you at this time. You may go. Please ask Lady Hawthorne if she will come in."

The detectives stood when Lady Hawthorne entered. She took a seat close to the fire, and asked them to please be seated. She appeared to be in her early forties, slender and graceful, with a no-nonsense, but gracious demeanor. DCI Hughes admired her clear and smooth skin and the way her tawny hair was clipped short and loose. He thought she was the most self-contained woman he had ever met. He started the interview by telling her that they were investigating her mother's death; that there was something suspicious about it. He did not mention the anonymous phone call.

"My word!" she said. "It appeared to me to be a natural passing. She had for some weeks been going down."

"Kindly tell me about your relationship with your mother."

"We got on quite well. Mother always let the servants take it easy on Thursdays, and so, on Thursdays, I rode Nellie over with a casserole for mother's supper. Mother and I would sit and reminisce for an hour or so, then I would ride home. I live but a mile from here."

"When did you last bring supper?" Hughes asked.

"Thursday week. I brought a quiche that I asked Mrs. Ward to heat. Sadly, mother could only take a few bites, she was too ill to have an appetite. I took the remainder of the quiche home. My husband, Lord Hawthorne, had it for a late supper."

Sergeant Turner decided against taking notes in front of Lady Hawthorne. His ears were tuned though, for any significant remark, and his eyes watched for any pertinent or odd signal that Lady Hawthorne might show. He had much to discuss later with Hughes.

"Do you have *any* notion about what affected your mother's health?" DCI Hughes asked.

"I have no idea. Her staff has been with her most of our lives, forty years, or so. Quite trusted. Not one of them would have given mother anything to make her ill."

There was a knock on the library door. Lady Hawthorne said come in. Mrs. Ward entered carrying a tray of tea and cakes.

The detectives relaxed while Lady Hawthorne poured out. DCI Hughes observed that as she drank her tea, Lady Hawthorne's hand shook slightly so that her cup rattled in its saucer, not in itself a sign of guilt. There could be many reasons for her nervousness.

As it broke through the gray mist that hovered outside, late sun flashed yellow stripes through the cut-glass windows and across the Persian carpet. Although it was a safe village, DCI Hughes did not want to be responsible for Lady Hawthorne's riding home in the dark, especially in this raw weather. He had a few more questions, then he would let her go.

"Can you tell us something about your sister?" he asked. "How did she get along with Lady Harrod?"

"For the last two years or so she and my mother have had their problems. Jane is wild but harmless. After she made a hasty marriage that the family warned her not to go into, and soon was pregnant with my nephew, Nigel . . . her husband, Lord Stuart, decided the marriage wasn't to his liking and moved to London. Without Jane. Jane has her own money left to her in a trust by our late father, but she soon goes through it each month, then comes up short."

Lady Hawthorne took a sip of tea and touched her napkin to her mouth. She selected a cake. The men waited. "Our mother tired of

Jane's asking for money. She told me she was stopping Jane's financial assistance . . . would see whether Jane loved *her*, or her open purse. Jane's the pretty one in the family; was always made a fuss over with her long silky hair. After her husband left, she turned into something of a flirt; she runs around imprudently. We hear gossip. I think she is trying to arouse her husband's jealousy. It doesn't work."

Lady Hawthorne thought perhaps she had said too much.

DCI Hughes shifted his feet and made mental notes. He watched the weak shadows lengthen across the carpet.

"I'll let you go now, so you can ride home with the remaining daylight. But one more question before you go . . . why is young Lord Nigel living here with his grandmother, instead of with his mother?"

"Well, you can best find that out from Lord Nigel." Lady Hawthorne hesitated, flicked her gaze around while deciding how much to say, how much not to say. "After her husband left, and Jane wanted more freedom, she sent Nigel here to live with mother. Mother has this large house, full of help, and when mother found that she had to pay for Nigel's college, she decided that he might as well live here. Then she could keep an eye on him; his mother wasn't. But no one has had influence over him and when he is home on holiday, he is often off somewhere; no one knows where. Running around with Lydia Jones, I dare say. I'm sure he has tried to keep Lydia a secret because the family, especially mother, deplores that young woman and her crass manners."

"But I understand that he was much beloved by Lady Harrod," DCI Hughes said, "and that when he was home, helped her in the gardens and orchards."

"Right. That's quite true. Mother loved him for that. It's surprising, with his being a loose cannon, that he was willing to do that; to stand still long enough. The estate has a grape arbor, quince trees, apple trees, peach . . . her favorite. He particularly tends the peach orchard . . . mother's prize, from which we make many ribbon-winning pies."

After the funeral, Lady Stuart, who lived in Tisbury, refused to come back out to the Harrod homestead. If DCI Hughes wanted to interrogate her, he bloody well could come to her, she warned.

He did. He brought Sergeant Turner with him. They enjoyed the clear, crisp day motoring out past the softly rounding fields. When they arrived at Lady Stuart's cottage, they had to knock several times before someone answered the door. A housemaid, wearing a crisp white apron over black silk, opened for them.

"Wait here," she ordered, as she let them in and closed the door behind them. "I'll see whether Lady Stuart is at home."

She had bloody well better be, DCI Hughes thought, as he and Sergeant Turner restlessly stood in the entryway, hats in hand.

The housemaid disappeared upstairs. In a few minutes she returned and showed the men into a parlor on the left side of the entry hall. "Lady Stuart will be with you shortly," she said. And without asking the men to be seated, she disappeared again.

DCI Hughes and Sergeant Turner waited, warming themselves by the fire. After ten-minutes Lady Stuart made her appearance. The men's' first impression of her was of a beautiful blonde-haired woman wearing too much lipstick and eye shadow. Her hair was piled into a mess of curls on top of her head, and, accidentally, or perhaps on purpose, a few curls had been pulled down around her face. She was dressed in a clinging, gray silk dress, hemmed just above her shapely knees, and an orchid-colored scarf was draped around her shoulders and down her back. On her feet were orchid silk, spiked sandals; hardly suitable for this weather. Hughes and Turner swapped glances. Hughes wondered whether this was typical for her, or whether she had *put on* for their benefit. In either case, she was sadly misguided.

They had been standing awkwardly, uncertain what move to make when finally she said, "Please sit and get on with it. I really have nothing to say. My mother grew ill, died, and we get on with our lives. Full stop."

"Lady Stuart, we think someone may have made a contribution to her death. You might have heard that we were alerted that something untoward may have happened to her, and an emergency warrant allowed us to take a blood sample as soon as her body arrived at the funeral home. Forensics found cyanide in her blood. As you may know, cyanide used to be an ingredient in rat poison, but has now been removed from the general market." He was pushing, but he wanted to scare her into cooperating. "Word has it," he said, "that for the past two years, you and your mother had a strained relationship. Can you tell us about that?"

"Well, I certainly couldn't have had anything to do with her death. I hardly saw her. You might ask my sister, Lady Hawthorne. She was closer to mother. Mother favored my sister. I got short shrift."

"When was the last time you *did* see Lady Harrod?" Hughes asked.

"I don't even know. Probably a month ago when I took jelly to her that cook made. It was jelly made from mother's quinces. I tried to be on her good side."

"We've been told that you were annoyed with Lady Harrod because she cut off your extra money. Is this true?"

"Well, you might say that . . . but you need to understand that I had a large inheritance coming from her as it was. She was old. How much longer would she live? Why would I fall out with her over money?"

Sergeant Turner wrote in his notebook; it seemed okay to do so in front of Lady Stuart. She was not as formal as Lady Hawthorne had been, and, she ignored him.

"Does your son, Lord Nigel, live with you?" DCI Hughes knew the answer, but he wanted her version; wanted to lead her onto the topic.

Lady Stuart's features pulled a smug sneer. "You must know by now . . . that he lives at Harrod Manor with my mother. She has a house full of servants to help, and I have only two."

Oh, your poor thing, Sergeant Turner thought, chin up and eyes lowered, picturing his wife at home doing the laundry and cooking, and at the same time—with no servant—refereeing two noisy children.

"Has Lord Nigel been here to see you recently?" Hughes asked.

Lady Stuart's defenses were up. "Of course not. I saw him at the funeral," but she felt pressure to volunteer more. "He's up at college now. He's reading chemistry and horticulture. In those disciplines, it was to his benefit to live with his grandmother. He helped with her gardens and orchards, and practiced his studies among her plants. I couldn't get along with her, but he did . . . capitally." She drummed her fingers on the walnut chair arm. Her scowl said *Will these insufferable men ever leave?*

DCI Hughes thought she appeared torn between flirting and wanting them out. Certainly, he mused, she would not offer tea or sherry, and would answer as few questions as possible. "I have no more questions for now, but we may want to speak with you again, Lady Stuart. You have been so kind. Thank you." She may not be able to be gracious, he thought, but he could be.

The detectives took their leave. It was a relief to get away from Lady Jane Stuart's hostility, and as they drove in silence back to headquarters, they compared their impressions of the strange woman. Sergeant Turner had a report to type and DCI Hughes wanted to read it—after typing.

"I could never make out your scribbles," he said to Turner.

Before going their separate ways, they stopped for a pint at the Black Tooth to discuss the case. Tomorrow they would start with Lady Harrod's housekeeper, Mrs. Ward.

On his drive home Hughes again tried Alena's number. No answer. Now he *was* anxious about her welfare.

DCI Hughes introduced himself and Sergeant Turner, and they stood until Mrs. Ward took a seat.

"Now gentlemen, how can I help?" she asked.

"Tell us, please, whatever you can think of, that might have led to Lady Harrod's illness." DCI Hughes wished he could relieve some of the sadness evident in Mrs. Ward's eyes. "We'll try to be brief. I know this is painful, Mrs. Ward."

"Indeed, sir, it isn't the same around here without Lady Harrod."

The housekeeper had invited the men back to her sitting room off the butler's pantry. She asked that sherry be served them, and presently a housemaid brought in a tray on which stood a decanter of sherry and three glasses. Sergeant Turner wrote in his notes that Mrs. Ward appeared sad, but relaxed, and, just possibly this was an occasion for her to get off her tired feet. This was a large manor to manage.

"Couldn't it have been a normal cause? I can't imagine anything untoward," she said. "Everyone here loved her. It's true that she had problems with Lady Stuart, but Lady Stuart stayed away for the most part. Recently she brought Lady Harrod jelly, made from quinces that grew here, but that seems innocent enough. The kitchen rumor was that she had frequently asked Lady Harrod to sweeten her coffers; a big spender she was, sir, and Lady Harrod finally said *no*. We heard some raised voices. But, it seemed to me that Lady Stuart accepted her mother's final refusal. Lady Stuart's son, Lord Nigel, lives here and Lady Harrod, we all know, paid for his upkeep and college. So Lady Stuart has had nothing to complain about."

"Could you provide us with a sample of the jelly, Mrs. Ward?" Hughes asked.

"Of course, sir."

She pulled a rope that hung nearby and presently there was a knock at the door. She gave instructions to the maid, who left, shutting the door softly behind her. Shortly the maid returned and handed Mrs. Ward a jar that appeared to contain jelly. Mrs. Ward handed it to DCI Hughes, who handed it to Sergeant Turner.

"How does Lord Nigel get along with the staff?" Hughes continued.

"He is a flirt, sir. He charms everyone. Wraps us around his finger. He really had Lady Harrod hooked. He helped her in the gardens every time he came home. Spoiled, he is. But charming. He . . . ."

The room was quiet with expectation.

"Yes, do go on," DCI Hughes gently prodded.

"Well, he keeps bringing around his lady friend, a Miss Lydia Jones. He brings her in the back entrance; hides her from his grandmother. Miss Jones has him in her thrall. Rules him. And she is not the type to fit into this household, if you know what I mean. If you'll excuse my saying so . . . a real sex pot . . . and loud. Not that the other Harrod women are not attractive, but they don't advertise it like Miss Jones does."

Hughes had to suppress an image of Lady Stuart's spiked sandals and short skirt. He waited for Mrs. Ward to consider what she wanted to say next.

"We downstairs heard them arguing. Miss Jones demanded that she and Lord Nigel marry secretly, and he told her that until his inheritance came in from Lady Harrod, he could not afford to marry. And he could not bring her to live here. He said his grandmother wouldn't hear of it." Mrs. Ward suddenly felt uncomfortable and adjusted her shawl to keep her hands busy. She knew it was necessary, but she didn't like discussing the family with strangers.

Dinner aromas wafted from the kitchen nearby. Sergeant Turner began to think about his wife's good cooking and how soon he could get to it.

"Lord Nigel thinks he will take a first in chemistry," Mrs. Ward said. "A clever lad if there ever was one. And with his education about plants, he has turned Lady Harrod's scraggly peach orchard into a winner. He's a bit barmy though . . . the dedication he has, working through the heat most of the summer. This fall, we cooked peach pies every week. Sad that he has to be mixed up with that vixen, Miss Lydia Jones."

"Right," DCI Hughes said.

"I heard him tell her to be patient he would work out something. The staff knew Lady Harrod would be so disappointed if he married Miss Jones, for she intended her grandson to marry our neighbor and longtime family friend, Miss Prentiss Wright. Miss Wright is every bit as attractive as Miss Jones . . . just doesn't flaunt it so. Lord Nigel is plain blind."

"How do you mean, Mrs. Ward? Blind in which way?" DCI Hughes asked.

"They grew up so close together that he thinks of Miss Wright in a sisterly way, no doubt. He's made it clear to everyone except Lady Harrod, that he has no intention to marry Miss Wright. Sad, sir. Everyone could see Miss Wright's fancy for Lord Nigel."

"Mrs. Ward, what do you think will happen to Harrod Manor now?"

"We've been told that Lord and Lady Hawthorne will occupy, sir. Lady Hawthorne grew up here, and she's the next in line. Of course we'll have to see whether Lord Nigel will stay here with them. I don't think he wants to live with his mother, Lady Stuart."

The sounds from the kitchen of rattling pots and dishes warned Hughes that it was growing late.

"Mrs. Ward, you've been most helpful," he said. "There's one more item you might help us with."

"Of course."

"If you can spare the time now, please show us to the greenhouse and the gardens Lady Harrod tended."

Mrs. Ward walked out with them to the kitchen gate and pointed them in the right direction.

In the greenhouse, Sergeant Turner examined the compost shredder and the remains of ground-up material beneath it, as DCI Hughes examined Lady Harrod's and Lord Nigel's gardening shoes; a whitish dust around them had caught his attention. He took the shoes over to the window to examine more clearly. Then he put them into a plastic bag that he drew from his pocket, and walked over to watch his sergeant who was scooping up and bagging some of the fine powder and peach pits that lay under the shredder.

At Queen's College, Lord Nigel's tutor, Master Quinn, agreed to meet with the detectives. Quinn sat, legs crossed at the knee, cigarette in the air. His eyes, peering from his finely-chiseled face, appeared to be sizing up the detectives as they discussed Lord Nigel. Off to the right a fire blazed in an ornately tiled fireplace.

"No doubt, Master Quinn, you've heard about Lord Nigel's grandmother's death," DCI Hughes began.

"Indeed. Surely a tragedy. But, Lord Nigel is holding up well. He just returned from the funeral, and he'll be going back home for the holidays. Lady Harrod was elderly, I understand. Not too early for the old gal to bag it in."

Eyes rounded, the detectives gave each other a look.

"What sort is Lord Nigel?" asked DCI Hughes.

"Lord Nigel is my most ambitious student," Quinn said. "He is always experimenting in the chem lab. He's made several fine horticultural compounds this semester. When many of the other lads will be out rowing, Lord Nigel is usually studying and testing in the lab. He has been fortunate to be able to grow some unusual and rare plants in Lady Harrod's gardens, and is working on crossbreeding for their improvement." Master Quinn tapped his cigarette into a silver ashtray that sat on the cherry table at his side. "I called to see whether he can meet with you, but his porter said he isn't available. I checked the lab; it's one of those rare times when I don't know where he is." He drew on the cigarette, and through the curl of smoke, squinted at the men facing him.

The inquisition had been completed; the interrogations had been completed, and now DCI Hughes had terrible news to convey to the family and staff of Harrod Manor. He had called a meeting for this purpose. Both Lady and Lord Hawthorne were present, as well as Lady Stuart, and they sat waiting, sad, but composed. The staff, circling around the room, anticipated the worst as though a new horror was about to descend on the manor.

"What I'm about to relate to you is indeed sad news," DCI Hughes said. "Using peach pits, Lord Nigel apparently extracted an amazing concentration of cyanide. Undetected, he was able to use the chemistry laboratory at his school for this purpose. Forensics found cyanide in a sample of the whitish dust that I collected from Lady Harrod's gardening shoes. She was being poisoned so slowly that it would not be apparent to anyone."

Lady Harrod's daughters took the news quietly, not really understanding, or believing, but gasps of horror waved through the staff.

"And with the large amount of dust about the greenhouse due to Lord Nigel's grinding up compost, Lady Harrod would have thought nothing of a bit of dust in her shoes.

"Formerly used as rat poison, cyanide is no longer available on the open market," DCI Hughes continued after a pause to allow the group to absorb his dire news. "But Lord Nigel could grind his own without drawing attention—peach pits make good fertilizer and, with the proper lab equipment, as I said, he could extract cyanide. If anyone at Harrod Manor asked, he could say he was making fertilizer. Recycling. He loved his grandmother, but she was old and had not so many years left. The call of his inheritance, and the pressure to marry Miss Jones, misled Lord Nigel into forcing an early end to Lady Harrod's years."

The only sounds in the room now were occasional subdued sobs, and phrases such as, "I can't believe it," or, "I never!"

Then by way of further explanation, DCI Hughes said, "I was curious about the powdered residue found in Lady Harrod's gardening shoes, but not in Lord Nigel's, and I soon determined that during each trip home, Lord Nigel had sprinkled some of this powder in his grandmother's gardening shoes. Absorbing cyanide through the dermis of her feet killed her. Slowly. The pressure put on Lord Nigel by Miss Lydia Jones prevented his right thinking, and he had found an easy way to end Lady Harrod's life. After all, he reasoned, she was ancient, which made it seem like something of a lesser crime."

Driving home from the meeting at the manor, DCI Hughes once more tried Alena's phone. She answered.

"Alena, thank goodness I've finally reached you. I've been trying to all week."

"I took a quick trip to the U.S. I like to visit my aunt every two or three years. It's good to have a long chat with her from time to time; especially when I need leveling advice. Dear Larry, I'm *so* glad you phoned."

"But not letting me know where you were . . . what if something had happened to you . . . I would never have known."

"Aunt Nell would have reached you."

He felt renewed warmth at the knowledge that Alena must have been speaking to her Aunt Nell about him. "Well, you're back safe and I've thought of a solution to our housing needs. I've missed you so much I would put my office in a dirt cellar to be with you, but I hope we can find better common ground. Actually, it's the *ground* I'm calling about," he teased. He felt much better knowing Alena was all right. "My solution is this: let's seriously consider buying the cottage with an office and then putting in a kennel for Oscar. There's plenty of space in the back lawn to put one large enough for him to run. We can camouflage it with bushes."

During the long pause that followed, Hughes held his breath. Living without Alena would color his world black in short order. It had, he feared already begun to look gray.

"I love that idea," Alena said. "To end this standoff, I think I would have trained Oscar to a life running on a treadmill."

As Hughes drove home the gray skies looked pink and rosy, and anyone who could listen would have heard him humming a tune. Sometimes life was a grim struggle and sometimes it was terrific. Time for him to have the terrific one.

When news about the crime at Harrod Manor spread about, Lady Stuart was the sole family member who consented to be interviewed by the press, and she was especially dolled out for the cameras; more makeup than usual, for she knew how washed out those flashes would make one. When they asked her how these horrific events had affected her, she said, "Actually, I don't believe any of it; mother was quite old, you know. And my son, Nigel is highly moral." She had had to stretch to find this complement.

In time, Lord Nigel was transported to jail where he would have a long time to enjoy the special foods that his mother, and Lady Abigail Hawthorne, and Mrs. Ward brought to him; and a long time to read the chemistry and horticulture books Prentiss Wright brought; and a long time to wonder why he had no visits from Miss Lydia Jones.

The quince jelly contained quince and sugar and pectin and nothing else. Headquarters devoured it.

A Murder on Rolling Rock Road

Before the phone rang, Detective Andy McRae was in a deep sleep, having spent the last few nights sleepless. Roughly a year ago his wife had moved out, saying she was tired of living with a detective and his weird hours—didn't want that lifestyle anymore. In short, over the ten years of their marriage, they had grown apart. Maybe she had a lover. Andy hadn't cared to find out; she was gone. He had grown used to being alone—that is, until seeing her with a man in a restaurant three days ago. She still looked good.

The ringing seemed louder now, and it was

not part of a dream. Well, that was his life; at last get some sleep and the phone rings. He rolled over in disbelief and pulled the pillow over his ears. Flicker, Andy's cat, who also had been in a deep sleep, let out a complaining meow. But the ringing continued. Detective McRae swung his legs over the side of the bed and scrambled around in the dark for the phone. When he found it, he said into it, "Yeah?" Managing to open his eyes, he noticed the lighted clock sporting the awful hour of 1:00 a.m. Even the clock looks shocked and tired, he thought.

He attempted to absorb the information coming from the voice on the other end of the line—a fatality on Rolling Rock Road.

"Well, all right," he said, setting down the phone. "I guess that's it, Flicker." He stroked the cat's back, rudely interrupting its grooming. "You know the drill, Flicker." McRae roused himself enough to rub his eyes, sit up, and pull his body upright to stand. "Flicker, you don't know how lucky you are. All you have to do is lie around, groom, and eat. Oh, yeah . . . poop, also." Flicker swatted his long tail in recognition of his pampered life.

McRae pulled on warm pants, a flannel shirt, and a windbreaker against the chilly night. He grabbed his shoulder holster, dropped food and water into Flicker's dishes, scooped

Flicker's box, and headed out into the cold night.

At 4206 Rolling Rock Road, the horror of the crushed body, twisted into an unnatural position, churned McRae's stomach. He ought to be used to it by now, he thought. Freya Hanson, forty-year-old wife of Lars Hanson, had fallen through the banister lining their upper hallway. The body had multiple bruises, including some on the neck. The banister had several broken pieces and two jagged palings were lying on the entry floor. When McRae examined the banister, he found it sturdy and well made. It would have taken a lot of force to break through—much more force than someone simply bumping into it.

Observing the crime techs at work, and the photographer recording the scene, McRae stood back and made a few notes in the small notebook he had pulled from a pocket. He asked a tech which family members were in the house, and was directed to the kitchen where he found the deceased's husband, Lars Hanson, sitting at the kitchen table, trying to stay out of the way. Lars sat bent over, hands covering his face, and when he looked up at the detective coming into the room, McRae noted puffy eyes. McRae introduced himself, showed his badge, pulled out a chair, and turned it backward before straddling it.

"Please tell me what happened," McRae said.

"I found her like that when I came in," Lars said. "I don't know what happened."

"What time did you come in, and where had you been? And is there someone who can vouch for that?"

"I was at my Wednesday night poker group, and yes there were guys there who will verify that. I came in about midnight. I don't know when Freya came in . . . I think she also had gone out." Lars suppressed a sob and rattled on nervously. "She had a haircut this morning . . . said she would be going out to show it off. Sometimes on Wednesday when I'm at poker she would get together with her friends for a ladies' night." His shoulders slumped, his eyes were flame red, and it appeared to take a major effort to hold himself up.

"When I let the EMT's in I was surprised to find the front door unlocked . . . very unusual. I had come in through the garage, as we always do." He gestured toward the garage door. "Freya always checks the locks before she goes to bed, but after I found her on the floor and called 911, because an intruder could still be in the house, I checked the upstairs, and saw that the bed was still made. She had not gone to bed.

"I might add, Detective . . . it's painful for me to have to say . . . but it's not a secret to some of us, that she was having an affair with the guy across the street. Paul Winslow. I became suspicious a few weeks ago when I returned from poker and found two wineglasses forgotten in the sink. I asked Freya why two? And she said that when she poured the second glass, she had forgotten that she had already poured one. Then, also, I came in unexpectedly one night and found Freya in a dither, nervously trying to straighten herself, buttoning up and all. I wondered why she was embarrassed." A memory played out behind his eyes. "So for a few Wednesday nights, I waited in my car down the block, and on one of those nights, I saw Paul coming out of my house." Lars tightened his mouth into a sharp line before continuing. His chest heaved with short, jerky gasps.

Detective McRae nodded and waited quietly, giving him breathing space.

Lars paused to think about how much he wanted to say, and how much he wanted to leave unsaid. "I doubt that Sophia, Paul's wife, knows what's been going on some Wednesday nights when she goes to a mahjong group. She's the one with all the money in that marriage; controls the purse strings, and although Paul's been taking great risks, I don't think he wants to blow that comfortable situation. I've been biding my time waiting for that fling to wind down. But recently I gave

Freya an ultimatum . . . stop seeing Paul or I would confront the Winslow's and make sure that Sophia knew all about her husband's affair."

Lars stood, paced the floor, then leaned back on the kitchen counter. He worked at loosening his collar. His face was flushed. Detective McRae studied him. The horror was taking its toll on Lars. McRae finished his notes and told Lars to be sure to stick around. He said he would get back to him after he asked the neighbors whether they had seen or heard anything unusual during the night.

McRae then knocked at the house next door to ask what they might have witnessed. It was still in the wee hours, but he guessed that with all the police cars outside, no one would be asleep. Johanna Parker invited him in and freely answered his questions.

"Freya Hanson was odd . . . took liberties she shouldn't have taken," Johanna said. "I don't mind saying . . . it's well known, actually . . . that Freya could be irritating. She insulted people at random, behaved in unsuitable ways. I wished sometimes that I could see her coming, so that when she rang the bell, I could conveniently not answer the door. But, I can't imagine who would want to harm her."

Without meaning to let his mind wander, McRae admired Johanna's appearance. He flip-flopped between listening to her and watching how her tousled hair charmed him. It stood straight up in places.

"I know that she tried Lars, her husband's, patience." Johanna went on. "Occasionally I would hear them angrily shouting at each other. Lars was much older, you know, and I hate to say this, but the gossip is that Freya ignored him except when he fattened her bank account."

There was a long quiet space with only the sound of a clock ticking somewhere to remind McRae that, although it was pleasant listening to this woman's soft lilt, he had to get on with the investigation. He pulled his eyes away from Johanna and continued writing in his notebook. He folded it shut and looked up at her, waiting for her to continue. He noticed that her mouth turning up at the corners gave her a friendly look. Her skin was clear and lively even though she wore no makeup. Her pink robe looked so soft to the touch, McRae thought. She said she lived alone—and, she was quite at ease talking to him.

"Apparently there has been some neighborhood couples' dustup," she said. "I think both poor Freya and Sophia Winslow across the street had it in for Paul, Sophia's husband. It seems that everyone but Sophia knew that Paul was shagging Freya, and if that wasn't enough to create stress at my party last Saturday night, Paul flipped out over our new neighbor, Candy Foster. Candy makes men's blood boil and they behave irrationally around her—even the safely married. I had to stand back and laugh to myself. I'm an ad account executive, used to watching men stunned by beautiful women. And still I was surprised."

Johanna offered McRae something to drink: beer, coffee, soda, tea? "Hot tea would be great," he said. "Help keep me awake and warm." He looked toward the fireplace.

"If it weren't the middle of the night," she said, "I would build a fire." She went to the kitchen to put the kettle on.

"Please tell me more about your party," McRae called.

"It was Saturday night. Paul's interest in Candy was so obvious it was embarrassing," Johanna called back from the kitchen. "And clear that both Freya and Sophia were annoyed. They both were trying to devise ways to keep Paul, away from Candy." McRae moved to the kitchen doorway to watch Johanna and to listen.

"And I heard from a reliable source, that Freya was about to tell Sophia that she was having an affair with her husband," Johanna said. "I try to avoid the neighborhood gossip but it's a close-knit block, and they won't let me. Anyway, it's good to keep the neighborhood from dying of boredom," she stopped herself—almost about to laugh, "but certainly not when it might involve a death," she said on a more sober note.

She returned from the kitchen with a silver tray of tea and homemade cookies with white icing. "Keep your energy up for staying awake all night," she said as she poured their teas. She took a sip, and looked ready to say more. She waited for the detective to taste his tea, and then she continued. "They say that Freya wanted Paul to run off with her, to leave Sophia. Freya was so tired of Lars, even with his money. She barely hid her feelings. It's no secret that she married Lars for security. He's quite staid, you know, and Freya wanted to kick up her heels. She considered him dull. He's twenty years older than she is."

Detective McRae waited while she sipped tea; it gave him a moment to enjoy her without trying to puzzle the Freya-Paul-Sophia-Lars triangle.

"Lars is a wealthy man. He provided Freya with all kinds of luxuries and exotic trips. In return, she treated him badly. Some of us have wondered why he put up with it. On the other hand, apparently Freya guessed accurately that Sophia would toss Paul out if she found out he was philandering. So, in Freya's mind all she had to do was tell, and presto Paul was hers. She must not have realized just how modest was his financial situation. At least, this is the neighborhood storyline."

Johanna considered whether to say more. She flashed her eyes sideways at Detective McRae, and said, mischievously, "Some of us have noted that Paul and Freya have the perfect setup for an affair . . . at least on Wednesday nights when Sophia attends mahjong club and Lars is at poker. At least that's where they each claim they go."

Detective McRae thought that philandering was not an indicator of a tendency to murder, but he wrote something in his notebook. As they drank tea, Johanna gave him names of other neighbors to question the next day.

He thanked her for tea and for her help, and reluctantly said goodnight. Perhaps he could plan a way to see her again. He thought she was in her low forties. Anyway, she looked close to his forty-eight years. And he made a mental note that wouldn't be written in the notebook: he hadn't wanted to leave.

Thursday morning McRae directed his office to do research for any pertinent records for the Hanson's, as well as for their immediate neighbors. This research was to include phone records, and please get that to him ASAP. Still sleep deprived, but eager to question people while memories were fresh, and while waiting for reports from homicide, McRae called on the famous beauty, Candy, and her husband. Candy and Raymond Foster lived on the opposite side of the Hanson's house from Johanna.

"It's perfectly stunning to have just moved in and have a fatality next door," Raymond said.

"Extremely unpleasant, I'm sure," Detective McRae sympathized.

Raymond explained to the detective that they had moved in a week ago and were still unpacking, and he was to start his new job Monday.

"We went out for a hamburger last night, tired from unpacking and arranging, and collapsed into bed as soon as we got home. We heard nothing."

Candy seemed speechless, only cooing and nodding now and then in agreement with Raymond. Detective McRae verified for himself the assertion that she was a man trap. Well—not for him. Too much on the face and not enough behind it, he quickly decided. A porcelain and finely-sculpted face, grant you, and flaxen hair, but hollow underneath. He imagined that he could hear her head rattle. And that hair—she couldn't leave it alone; always flicking it back, then pulling it to the front.

"I must say . . . it's a tragedy and all that . . . that Freya met with that horrible accident," Raymond said, "but she was a strange, almost unwanted neighbor. On our moving day, not knowing the situation, or Freya's reputation, when she rang the doorbell ostensibly to welcome us to the neighborhood, we asked her in. Then she proceeded, uninvited, to examine the house all over, opening boxes, commenting on our possessions. Candy and I stood there, mouths agape. But would someone want to push her off a balcony because of bad manners?"

McRae scribbled a few notes. He had to get out of there before Candy again tossed her mane and gave it a few more twists over her shoulder. He might slip and say something she would not want to hear; such as, you could cut it off if it bothers you as much as your constant fiddling with it bothers me.

Later that afternoon Detective McRae drove to Paul Winslow's office and intercepted him just as he was about to leave. McRae flashed his badge and asked Mr. Winslow to wait a bit—he had a few questions.

"I can't absorb this yet. Can't believe it," Paul said. "And I know nothing about her accident." He ground a cigarette into an ashtray and pulled out car keys to indicate he was in a hurry. "I haven't seen Freya since Johanna Parker's party, Saturday. I admired Freya's new haircut and that was it. Yesterday, I stayed late at the office . . . had to email a report to my team for this morning's meeting. No one else was at the office to verify that, but the email will show the time stamp. When I got home about 10:00 yesterday evening, I ate the supper my wife, Sophia, had left warming for me while she was at her mahjong club. I watched a little TV and went to bed. When Sophia came in I was still awake and reading."

"Mr. Winslow," McRae said, "I've obtained Hanson's phone records and there's a call at 5:02 p.m. yesterday from Mrs. Freya Hanson's mobile to your office. What was that about?"

A surprised grimace flushed Paul's face for an instant. "Oh . . . uh . . . yes . . . Freya phoned. She wanted to know how I liked my new Mustang." A brilliant answer, Paul thought, since Freya wasn't available to deny or affirm. There was no reason, he thought, for the detective to know that Freya had called to issue new threats. Lately she had been increasing the pressure on him to leave Sophia, when all he had wanted was just an affair. Self-contained.

Leaving Winslow's office, McRae decided to stop off for lunch at The Greens diner. And while there take a few minutes to organize what he had learned; sort out some of the facts; ring his sergeant to get a warrant to extract Winslow's email, and last but not least, take a minute to plan something fun for himself. He had been working non-stop for months. Time for a rest. His thoughts strayed to Johanna.

The next day, unannounced, McRae stopped by the Winslow's house. He timed his visit after Paul had left for work, and before Sophia had had a chance to leave. At first she refused to answer questions, but had a change of heart after McRae said in that case she would have to come down to headquarters.

In responding to his questions, she seemed to think everything was normal—suspected nothing regarding her husband's affair with Freya; did not appear deeply disturbed about a suspicious fatality across the street. McRae knew that Paul had had time to warn her so they could agree to their facts. That was okay with McRae. Most of the time, he had his ways for getting at the truth.

"Apparently, when Freya fell through the banister, I was at mahjong," Sophia said. "Members of the club can vouch for that. When I got home sometime close to midnight, Paul was in bed reading. No . . . I hadn't heard or seen anything unusual across the street. Such a tragedy. Although at Johanna Parker's party, Saturday night, Freya was obviously hitting on my husband. When we got home, Paul and I had a shouting match about that, and he promised me he loved only me, and wouldn't think of straying to Freya . . . or to the new neighbor, Candy, who also was coming on to him," she laughed. "Having an attractive husband can rattle a marriage."

That evening, following up on his notes, Detective McRae knocked on Lars Hanson's door. When Lars opened the door, the detective said, "I'm so sorry to have to question you further at this terrible time, Mr. Hanson, but my department is after me to solve this case. And I have a few more questions."

Lars invited him in. He took the detective's jacket and asked him to have a seat. Then Lars stepped over to close the door that led into the family room, but not before McRae saw two large suitcases looking ready to go.

"Mr. Hanson, are you taking a holiday to give your heart a rest after your tragedy?"

"Indeed," Lars said, and he volunteered no more information.

"Mr. Hanson," McRae deliberately took his time holding up Lars and watching him squirm a bit. "Why would Mrs. Hanson have called Paul Winslow at his office on the day she fell?"

Lars appeared to be giving the question heavy consideration. "I can't imagine," he said. "Perhaps to arrange another tryst. Somehow they managed to get together."

"Have you had any contact with Sophia or Paul Winslow since Freya's fall?"

"No. None at all . . . they're not really in my good graces."

"I guess you've forgotten . . . but it's understandable in view of your tragedy. We've traced all pertinent phone records to determine who has been interacting with whom, especially in your immediate neighborhood, and your records show a twenty-minute call this morning to your number from Mrs. Sophia Winslow's line. Can you tell me what that's about?"

"Oh, uh, yes." Lars slapped his cheek, mouth agape, then laughed. "I recall now that Sophia called to express how sorry she was for Freya's tragedy. Everyone will miss Freya," he said almost in a whine.

Huh, McRae thought, not according to what he had heard.

Lars Hanson clearly was nervous —anxious to get McRae out the door, but the detective sat there expecting something more. He watched Lars fidget, first with his collar, then with his fingers, then scratching his scalp. He's hiding plenty, McRae thought.

Lars's gaze darted around the room. What could he do to get the detective out? Finally, he said, "Detective, can I offer you a drink?" Not what he wanted to do, but the loud pauses were killing him; he had to make a move of some kind.

There is much to learn here, McRae thought, but it would not happen now. He would wait and watch. "No, thank you," he said finally. "I'll be on my way." He watched Lars's body visibly relax into a deep breath.

Spring was undecided whether to relent and warm up, or to keep its children in a chill. At the moment, chill reigned and as he headed home, Detective McRae turned up the heat in his regulation police transportation. Boring, but necessary to have a nondescript automobile, he thought. Maybe he would look into a Mustang for himself. It would be fun to take that lovely woman, Johanna Parker, out in a spiffy new red Mustang. If she would go. He had spent hours chilled in that police ride observing Rolling Rock Road to see what went on; get an idea of who was with whom. Some shadowy movements took place in the dark, but Johanna Parker's house was always quiet. No one coming or going. He wasn't spying on her—she just happened to be the next door neighbor to the accident. It went with the territory. And his confidence grew that she would be free to go out with him. He would ask her soon. First, get a little space from the investigation.

Friday, late afternoon, Paul Winslow opened his door to find Detective McRae and his sergeant. From an upstairs window, Sophia had seen the police arrive. She would not go down; let Paul deal with them. After quoting the Miranda warning to Paul, McRae said, "Mr.

Winslow, you said you hadn't seen Freya Hanson since Johanna Parker's party Saturday night, when you told her that you liked her new haircut. But, she did not get her haircut until the following Wednesday, the day she died. I'm taking you in for further questioning. I believe that you met Mrs. Hanson Wednesday night when your wife was at her mahjong club, and Lars Hanson was at poker.

Paul seemed to collapse into himself. There was no further explaining he could offer now. He had no reply and turned away from McRae, so he did not have to face him.

The detective continued speaking to Paul's back. "Telephone records show that Mrs. Hanson called your office and may have threatened to tell your wife about your affair. Witnesses have come forward to verify that Mrs. Hanson wanted to leave her husband and go off with you, and that she was tired of waiting. What she did not know was that you would be nearly penniless without your wife's income.

"So, you must have agreed to meet her at her house," McRae continued. "And then, when she couldn't be talked out of her threat, you could not control your rage, and fought with her. There were bruises on her neck. She may have tried to get downstairs but you pushed her through the banister, perhaps not on purpose. Then, in a panic, you left through the front door, which left it unlocked . . . a door that was never left unlocked. You knew you could not afford a divorce, and could not afford Freya Hanson's expensive habits. And, it is probable that your wife would kick you out if she learned about your affair."

Detective McRae watched Paul Winslow squirm with panic like a trapped wild animal. His shoulders rounded into his chest. Then he straightened up and turned to face McRae. He looked a bit brighter. "But, I have the timestamp on the emailed report that will prove I was at the office when Freya took her fall," Paul said. "Besides, she could be disagreeable . . . not someone I would spend much time with."

"Our tech group has verified that your email was pre-programmed to be sent at a specific time," McRae said. "So that is not in itself proof."

Ah, well, he wouldn't get to see that pretty thing, Candy, again, Paul thought, as he got in the police car. However, though he had not killed Freya Hanson, he was relieved to have her off his back.

After she watched Paul ride off, Sophia dialed Lars's number. "He's gone," she said.

Soon, on a dark night, a quarter-block down Rolling Rock Road from the Hanson's, Detective McRae parked under an old maple tree. Once more in the chill, he waited and watched until late one night he saw a car exit from the Hanson garage, and without turning on the headlights, the car backed straight across the street into the Winslow's driveway. Then the auto's trunk popped open. By the moonlight, McRae saw a figure exit from the car, go to the Winslow's door, saw the front door open, and a figure appear in the lighted doorway. He saw what looked like suitcases being loaded into Hanson's car. Then it drove away.

Guilty. But of murder? That was the big 24-karat question, McRae thought. Depressing. Not surprising. Better to think forward to tomorrow night and the date with Johanna Parker. Tomorrow, he mused, he will deck out in some new threads, pull the new Mustang from his garage, and at 6:10 sharp, knock on Johanna's door. She had said she would love to have dinner with him; he pictured that up-turned mouth. And she had called him Andy.

The Green Valley
Painting Club Murder

"**D**etective, we have a situation the hospital thinks should be looked into," Dr. Seaugut said. "Quietly. We don't want to cause a panic but we regard this as urgent. We found a lethally high concentration of thallium in the urine of a woman, Libby Bonneville, who came in by ambulance last night and died shortly after." The doctor was calling from Green Valley Regional Hospital.

When Dr. Seaugut's phone call came, Detective Logan Walker had just been settling down with his newspaper and morning wake-up coffee.

"We don't want our good citizens to think it's something in the water," the doctor said. "That's why we called you first, detective, as you work privately and were highly recommended. We trust you can find the source before the news gets about."

Detective Walker agreed to meet the doctor at the hospital within the hour, and he and his associate, Detective Clive Parker, now sat facing Dr. Seaugut across his desk. Off to the side sat the hospital director, Mr. Giles Trayfort. The good doctor explained a little about thallium.

"Gentlemen, I'm sure you know that, once used in rat poison, thallium's no longer available on the general market. There are antidotes, if caught in time, but unfortunately Mrs. Bonneville's dose was either too concentrated, or she didn't get here in time for us to determine the problem and administer the antidote." He scribbled something on a pad and handed it to Detective Walker.

"This is her address. We don't think it's a case for the police yet, but if you find anything suspicious, of course we'll call them. We need to find out first, where she got the thallium. Her husband, Larry Bonneville, is certainly distraught and he has no idea what happened to his wife. He came in with the ambulance, and I had to medicate him to help calm him. I don't suspect foul play from him. But you never know. Something went wrong with Libby Bonneville." The doctor shuffled papers around on his desk and then stood—a signal that the interview was over and he had to get back to his patients. "You don't have to be concerned with Bonneville children, as there are none."

Up to this point Mr. Trayfort had not spoken, merely giving nods of agreement, but now he said, "The hospital wants to keep this quiet until we know where the thallium came from. I'm certain that in your profession you are used to being discrete."

"I understand," Walker said. "I assure you of our discretion. And Detective Parker and I will start right away by talking to Mr. Bonneville."

When there was no answer at the Bonnevilles' door, Detective Walker walked around back and found Larry Bonneville sitting in his back garden, staring off into space— looking more dead than alive. He seemed eager to talk.

"When Libby arrived home yesterday from painting at the artists' clubhouse, she was nauseous and dizzy. She stumbled into the house and I called to her, 'What's wrong, hon?' But before she could say anything, she started flailing her arms and dropped to the floor thrashing about and moaning. I immediately called 911 for an ambulance. Except for a cold now and then, she's never been sick." Larry

Bonneville, a thin man to begin, looked as though he could not provide the will to brace against the breeze.

"A terrible thing," Detective Walker said. "I empathize with how you must feel."

"Sadly, I've been angry with Libby lately . . . she was painting too much at home. Why did she have to make a mess here and expose us to those fumes, when she could paint at the clubhouse where there is proper ventilation to deal with it?" Larry struggled to deal with the tragedy and his loss, as well as his anger. "I'd let her cover the walls with paint if that would bring her back. It will not be easy adjusting to living without her. I keep expecting her to come around the corner any minute." He slammed his fist down on the chair arm. "She had been so elated to win the state blue ribbon . . . and now this."

Detective Walker indeed knew how Mr. Bonneville felt; he himself had had to adjust to living alone after his wife died a year ago. She had been ill for many years, though, and so he had had time to adjust to it, but still it was a great loss.

For a minute, Larry Bonneville couldn't continue. He threw his head back and shut his eyes against the horror. He pulled in long streams of breath, working for control. Detective Walker waited quietly. "The doctor said it appeared to be thallium poisoning,"

Larry said. "I don't even know what thallium is. Where would Libby have gotten thallium?"

Detective Parker, used to letting Walker run interrogations, kept quiet, but his face clearly showed sympathy.

"I don't know myself but I intend to find out," Detective Walker said. "We'll be questioning the artists who use the clubhouse. We'll need that address, and a name to contact."

Detective Walker next called on Anne Black, President of the Green Valley Painting Club. When he explained why he was there, and Anne had examined his badge, she invited him to step in and follow her back to the kitchen where she was in the middle of cleaning brushes. She wore vinyl gloves and an apron that showed evidence of many sessions next to a paint-filled brush.

"I hope you don't mind that I finish up here," Anne said. "Libby's death is a terrible shock, and I have to keep busy so that it doesn't get me down. Also, I've been away, and these brushes were left too long in Murphy's Oil Soap; caked up pretty hard and need work." She looked around at Detective Walker waiting patiently. "Please have a seat."

"We can talk while you work," he said, "I don't mind at all." and he pulled up a stool and sat at the breakfast bar, notebook and pen in hand.

"As you know, Libby was a member of our club. The news about this horrible misfortune has gone around fast, and we're all in a state of disbelief. Until lately, Libby painted with the group at our clubhouse. I haven't seen her recently because she was working more at home on a large canvas that she didn't want to haul around, and, I've been out of town the past week." She stood a few clean brushes in a jar, then picked up two more to soap. "That painting . . . she called it 'Vaporous Vespers', recently won the blue ribbon in an important statewide, juried show, and we were all so happy for her. She worked long and hard to improve her technique . . . and now this. What a shame."

"Can you think of anyone who resented Mrs. Bonneville, or may have wanted to cause her harm?" Walker asked.

Anne's mouth gaped open, she dropped a brush. She jumped to pick it up before the detective could. "You mean there's something suspicious about her death? We were all wondering about the cause . . . thought it might be food poisoning."

"No. This is a routine investigation, but we do want to question all who may have had contact with Mrs. Bonneville this past week." In keeping with the hospital's wishes, Walker wanted to allay fears, at least until there was evidence regarding the source of thallium.

Anne gave Walker a list of club members and their addresses—anyone who might have knowledge of Libby's activities during her last days.

"The club regulars all knew her and probably did have some contact with her the past week," Anne said. "Let's see . . . there're Abby Peters, and Emmett Sims; they work in oils. Sarah Greene, and Chloe Little, who work with acrylics or watercolors. And Doug Morrison, he's been away for the past two weeks visiting relatives. They're all usually painting at the clubhouse Monday through Thursday, and might have been there yesterday, but it's unlikely. Rarely does anyone go in on Friday. However, before I left for my trip, I heard Libby say that since fumes from her oil paints and turpentine were getting to Larry, she would be painting at the club more. She said she intended to come in every day until she finished a new painting she had started."

Anne's brow tensed into a frown as she absent-mindedly kept drying a brush that was already dry. Then she seemed to force herself to relax. "It's a congenial group," she added, "and even though we're competitive, we still laugh and have a good time painting together on occasion." She finished with the brushes, standing each one in a jar by the sink. As she poured ice teas for them, Detective Walker wrote in his notebook.

"Anything else you can think of about the club and its members," he said, "whatever comes to mind."

Anne mentally pictured the artists, wondering to herself what might be significant. "Well, take Emmett Sims He has a Master's of Fine Art in painting, and usually takes the blue ribbon . . . the same one that Libby just won in the statewide show. But he took his loss with dignity. He's our most dedicated artist. He even imports and grinds his own pigments. A purist. He does something unusual by making some of his pigments phosphorescent. Eye catching."

She took a sip of tea and leaned on her chin, thinking. Walker gave her plenty of quiet space in which to collect her thoughts.

"I hate to say this about poor Libby, but some of us had problems with her. She would borrow expensive paints or brushes . . . and not pay back. Abby in particular has complained about that. Libby had her irritating habits . . . often she would order a soda and let someone else pay for it. Just carelessness, I'm sure . . . the Bonnevilles were not hard up."

"Thank you Ms Black. This is helpful. We will be questioning everyone who used the clubhouse."

"I'm fairly certain no one will be there today, Saturday," Anne said, as she saw

Detective Walker out. "But as most of us are retired, you'll have no trouble reaching the members at home."

Emmett Sims, the oil painter who usually took the blue ribbon, was trimming bushes when Walker arrived. The detective parked in front of the house and strode across the finely trimmed lawn to the hedge where Emmett pruned. Walker held up his badge for Emmett to examine.

"Hello, Mr. Sims. I'm Detective Walker, and I'd like to ask you a few questions regarding Mrs. Libby Bonneville."

Emmett paused hedge-trimming long enough to squint up at the badge, then continued pruning as he reluctantly prepared himself to answer the detective's questions. He did not say hello or anything else, nor did he invite the detective inside.

"Mr. Sims, I'm sure you've heard that Libby Bonneville died suddenly last night. Because her condition was mysterious, the hospital called me to look into whatever she may have been exposed to. Can you tell me anything about the last time you saw Mrs. Bonneville?"

Emmett knew he was trapped; he reluctantly came out with the words, "Yes, I saw Libby at the clubhouse, Monday. She finished and signed another painting. She called it 'Wildwood.' Some might think it was a winner." He looked up from the hedge long enough to roll his eyes toward the sky. "She said she was happy to be done with it and would enter it in the next show."

"Did you see her yesterday?" the detective asked. "Mr. Bonneville said Libby came home from the clubhouse sick. Fatally sick."

"Of course, that's really too bad. What did I do yesterday? I attended a street fair in Patagonia. Sold three oils," Emmett said, chin up—just dare to question that, he thought. "Most of us don't go to the clubhouse on Fridays or weekends. We have other things to do, but maybe some of the others were there."

He yanked at the hedge as though punishing it for something mysterious.

"You might talk to Sarah Greene. I heard Sarah say that Anne Black, our president, complained to her about Libby's using everyone else's supplies." With this, he hoped to deflect attention away from himself. "Naturally, I would wish no harm on her, but Libby was one woman I avoided because she was always borrowing."

He looked up from the hedge and waved his hedge-trimmer in the air. "She never borrowed paint from me though. She tried to once and I said no. I told her how time-consuming it was to grind my own pigments."

Detective Walker, tired of standing around watching Emmett prune, finished his notes and pocketed his notebook. "Thank you, Mr. Sims. You've been most helpful." Exaggerating his good will, he left Emmett—who had no parting reply—to his hedge.

As he watched the detective drive away, Emmett continued attacking the bush, but he wasn't paying attention to pruning and hacked a great gash out of the hedge. Without looking back, he dropped the shears on the spot, and swearing to himself, he stomped into the house. Then he remembered to retrieve his calm nature and to relax. Nothing serious. Just a dumb guy who thinks he's Scotland Yard. Still, there were some precautions he must take.

It was only 1:00 p.m. and Detective Walker felt he had accomplished a good deal for the morning. Time for a quick lunch at a drive-up. As he sat eating in the Porsche, he thought over the ground he had covered so far: one distraught husband; one amiable painting club president; one surly artist who clearly did not want to be bothered. The list would get longer as a few names remained on his list of artists he had not questioned, and who might say something revealing. So far, nothing definite.

Next on his list was Sarah Greene and as he knocked at her door, he could hear a TV blaring from the back of the house. He knocked several times before she opened the door. He held up his badge, which she studied, scowling to show her annoyance at the interruption.

"Since when do detectives drive Porches?" She threw the words out, as she looked over his shoulder at the car.

"I'm undercover," he said. "I have to have a ride that won't attract attention," he teased.

"Humph," she growled.

"Ms Green, I must ask you a few questions about Libby Bonneville and the painting club. Don't worry, you're not being singled out . . . I'm interrogating all who had contact with Mrs. Bonneville."

Sarah had been loading the dishwasher and she headed back to the kitchen to continued to do so. If he chose, the detective could follow her back to the kitchen to stand and watch. On whose authority did he have permission to question her? she wanted to know.

"Green Valley Regional asked me to investigate the situation surrounding Libby's last days. Right now, I'm interested in the relationships between her and the club members." The detective found Sarah to be such a put-off, that he had to force himself to be straight with her.

She pulled a grimace of the sort that says: go away, you're bothering the bloody hell out of me. She wore a sloppy tee shirt with cutout sleeves barely covering her excessive flesh and grungy bra. She began to scrub one of the pots piled in the sink. From where the detective stood, the pots looked as though they had been stacked up for a week waiting for soap and water. The loud TV did not bother Sarah and she did not offer to turn it down.

"Actually, there was tension between all of us," she said, finally. "We all had been hoping to win the blue ribbon in the last show. No one said it, but it was in the air. It's the same every year." Her mind seemed to drift out the window as if seeing the past. The detective waited for her to bring it back to the present. She continued to lather a pot without offering him coffee, although she stopped scrubbing long enough to pour a cup for herself. She did not ask him to have a seat.

Nevertheless, he pulled out a chair, sat, and hooked his shoes on the rungs. Leaning on his elbows, he propped his chin on his fist and waited. He looked around at the clutter, and smelled the sour odor that pervaded her house. She needs to scrub more than that pot, he thought.

"Libby had such a big head from her recent blue ribbon," Sarah said, "that she was eager to finish up her new painting for the next show. She was under major stress and looked worried. She confided to me that she had had an argument with her husband, Larry, early in the week, and he had stormed out of the house.

116

Seems he had no patience with paint fumes in the house. So, I think she worked at the clubhouse every day this week."

"Did you paint at the clubhouse yesterday?" Walker asked.

"No. No one goes in on Friday. If I did, I'd be the only one there and that wouldn't be fun."

It might have been more fun for the others, though, Walker thought.

Sarah dried the pot and put it away.

Expecting her to open up and say more, Walker waited.

"Some of us would be happier if Libby painted at home. Anne Black, our president, complained to me recently that she had loaned Libby a brush that Libby conveniently forgot to return. And Libby often borrowed expensive paints without offering to replace them."

Walker couldn't get away from Ms Sarah Green fast enough. He hoped he'd gotten all she could add to his inquiry, and hoped that he wouldn't have to encounter her again. Times like this he gained some wisdom: it wasn't his choice to live alone, but it could be worse. The sun clocked in now with long late shadows; should he call it a day? Better push on—catch people while memories are fresh.

When Detective Walker knocked on Chloe Little's door, she invited him right in. "I didn't go to the clubhouse yesterday. It's rare for any of us to go in on Friday," Chloe said, in answer to the detective's question. "But I think Libby might have been there to finish the landscape she called 'Wildwood'. The last I saw it, it was moving along nicely and only needed a dab or two and Libby's signature. She said she would work on it all week. You know . . . oil paintings need drying time before they can be varnished and submitted to a show. No time to waste." Chloe poured glasses of sherry for them, and invited Walker to sit. She seemed pleasantly ready to settle back for a long chat.

He noticed that she did not wear a wedding ring; perhaps she lived alone. He also noticed that she was attractive, well groomed, and about his age. Moreover, her condominium was tidy—not cluttered like Sarah's—and had an alluring aroma of apples. And, most important, she had a lovely smile. Taking advantage of the opportunity to relax, Walker thought a minute about some of the questions he wanted to ask. "I'm hearing about tensions between Libby and the club members," he began. "Can you tell me what that's all about?"

"Ah yes, that is true. Some had trouble with Libby's frequent borrowing. She wasn't organized to have the right materials, and would borrow right and left, and we all knew that it wasn't for a lack of money." Chloe sipped sherry and thought for a minute about how much gossip to reveal. "Emmett Sims was sour because Libby took the blue ribbon in the last state-wide show. He tried not to show it, but his face had a permanent scowl and he had lost all sense of humor. He was spoiled . . . and used to winning. The behind-scenes gossip was that the prize, instead of going to Libby, belonged to those who had loaned her all their paints and brushes. That's a silly thought, of course." She waved her hand in a dismissive gesture. "Libby, though a lovely gal, did burn a few bridges."

Detective Walker wanted to linger with this pleasant woman, but duty called. He thanked her for her help and left.

Each of the club members Detective Walker questioned said they had not been at the clubhouse Friday. Doug Morrison said he and Abby Peters were supposed to meet to paint outdoors, but Abby hadn't shown up. "I know Libby wanted to finish 'Wildwood'," Doug said. "Most of us have other chores to do on Friday, but Libby might have gone to the clubhouse to finish it. She told some of us that her husband was snarly about her painting at home . . . didn't like the fumes."

As Detective Walker made his interview rounds, his associate, Clive Parker, detective in training and former police captain, had been working quietly behind the scenes. With the clubhouse key that Anne Black had supplied, he went in and searched the clubhouse for anything that might have traces of thallium. From the trash, he pulled soda cans and a few other items of potential interest: paint-covered paper towels, throwaway scrapers, and brushes, and put them into evidence bags for forensics.

Part of his assignment was to pick up a painting from each artist member of the Green Valley Painting Club. For this he had to have warrants which, considering that a potential murder was involved, the judge faxed to him immediately. Detective Parker also asked for warrants to search each artist's supplies—if needed. He had no problem sourcing the paintings until Saturday evening when he met with opposition from Emmett Sims, due to the preciousness of his hand-ground pigments. And Parker's instructions from Detective Walker were to be sure to get one of Mr. Sims's that had phosphorescent highlights. This had taken some doing—he had had to raise the intimidation level. But over the years, he had developed a formidable approach that came in handy when he needed to intimidate his opponent.

Good thing he had a van, for some of the paintings were huge. Yikes, he thought, he was glad he didn't have to look at them for longer than it took to drop them off; although a few were interesting and easy on the eyes. He knew nothing about art, but he knew what he liked.

Sunday night, after much driving all over, he dropped his evidence off at the forensic lab. Keep it quiet, he instructed the lab technicians.

But already by late Saturday, Emmett Sims had removed all traces of thallium from his home workshop. He had carefully packaged this, and rushing, had driven 45 miles to Tubac to deposit the package in a dumpster behind gift shops where several other dozen bags of trash waited. He dared fate to lead anyone specifically to his package. And when he was there, he window-shopped art galleries and had dinner lest anyone ask why he had gone to Tubac.

On Monday morning, having finished questioning all the artists on the list, Detective Walker and Detective Parker turned their evidence over to Green Valley Regional. They then knocked on Emmett Sims's door. When Emmett opened the door, Walker stepped in and read him the Miranda warning.

"Mr. Sims, we're taking you in for further questioning regarding the death of Libby Bonneville. You said that on last Monday you saw her finish and sign 'Wildwood', but according to her husband, it was not finished until Friday when she arrived home late with it . . . fatally sick. We believe you were at the clubhouse Friday. And we believe invoice records will show that when you imported pigments recently, you also ordered thallium with which you use to create your phosphorescent colors. We found traces of thallium in a soda can in the club's trash and we've lifted prints from the can. We weren't surprised to find yours and Libby's among them. She died of thallium poisoning, which we suspect that you, knowing that thallium is tasteless, put in a soda that, typically, she let you buy for her."

"But I wasn't at the club on Friday." Emmett announced.

"So you say. I expect that you can provide sales receipts for the paintings you said you sold in Patagonia on Friday."

Emmett sneered, his hands on his hips. "I didn't issue sales receipts."

"Well, Mr. Sims, Patagonia is such a small place, I'm sure we can find, with your help, your buyers."

Emmett did not reply but kept his sneer. His sense of dignity would not yield. He smirked as if to say you have to prove I was not in Patagonia.

When Emmett offered no reply Detective Walker said, "I have a warrant to search your records. And I wouldn't be surprised if we found thallium among your supplies, as well as packing slips listing thallium. But even if we don't, forensics has confirmed the use of thallium in the paint on your canvas. You couldn't stand losing the blue ribbon to Libby and you wanted to punish her and to make sure she never again won it. You mistakenly thought of that ribbon as yours. Since no one tended to come to the clubhouse on Friday, you felt assured no one would know you had been there, aside from Libby, who would go home too sick to discuss it."

As the police walked Emmett out, his thoughts were on how difficult it would be to win any more blue ribbons.

It wasn't many days until Detective Walker's thoughts were on Chloe Little. He knew she would be a good dinner companion to invite to a cozy bistro. And he knew of a cozy bistro. He hoped she was free; she had had such a warm, pretty smile.

A Naturopathic Death

The Madison Regional Hospital had called in Detective Peter Wilson when it began to appear that Tom Lewis's death was suspicious. What had happened to Tom wasn't clear.

"Tom's serum pH was skewed and perhaps it was that which had caused his liver to kill off his red blood cells," Dr. Sauvmor said. "Then, without enough red blood cells to supply hemoglobin to his heart, he had a heart attack for lack of oxygen. He just didn't get to the hospital in time for us to save him.

"Mr. Lewis's next of kin is his daughter, Sandy Bennett; you might start your investigation with her. However, Mr. Lewis's lady friend, Claire Johnson, is the one who called 911 for him."

Sandy Bennett lived at the water's edge of Madison down a long, dusty, point of land in a fragile cottage that leaned toward the beach as though trying to reach the sea. Avoiding waist-high weeds that would scrape both sides of his Mustang, Detective Wilson drove down the lane, maneuvering around potholes. With the sea sparkling before it, the cottage, when it came into view, appeared to have been washed up by the tide after drifting a few months. It reminded Wilson of the piglet with the house made of sticks. In a cloud of dust, he pulled up before the front steps.

Sandy eyed him from the porch where she sat smoking and rocking in an old paint-peeled rocking chair.

Well, she is up and dressed, he thought, as he climbed out of the Mustang, and held up his badge for her to see.

She said nothing, pulled air through her cigarette, flicked tobacco off her lip, and continued to eye him knowingly

He rose up the three unpainted, wooden and squeaky porch steps, taking in the potato sack shirt that hung over Sandy's baggy shorts. Pink flip-flops adorned her crusty feet.

Sandy kept rocking, eyes squinting through curls of smoke. She waited for him to speak.

"Miss Bennett, I have been assigned to investigate your father's death. I know what a shock it must be and how unsettling, but I must ask you a few questions." So far, the detective thought, Sandy did not appear to be consumed by grief.

"You are Sandy Bennett, are you not?"

She nodded toward the Mustang, took another drag on her cigarette, and squinted through the smoke. "Cool ride."

He ignored this remark.

She didn't offer him a seat. He helped himself to the swing next to her and sat down.

But now she had second thoughts about her demeanor, and she began to loosen up—it might be to her advantage. She tilted her head down, used her shirt to wipe her eyes, and said between sighs, "I don't know anything about my dad's death. I know only that his fiancée, Claire, called to tell me that he died. I hadn't seen him in a while . . . but I was planning to." She forced a deep and audible sob. "At least this will prevent his marrying Claire!"

Detective Wilson suppressed a laugh. "I'd be willing to guess it will," he said, rolling his eyes. She has not combed her hair in a week, he thought. Long and bushy, she had just pulled it up in back, letting it shag out.

Sandy used the rocking-chair arm to smudge out her cigarette. Then, from a pocket she removed chewing gum, unwrapped a stick, and not offering any to the detective, she mouthed it, crumpled the paper and tossed it over the bannister.

Wilson noticed other gum wrappers nearly swallowed up by high weeds.

In between the occasional sob, Sandy smacked gum, echoing the noise across the bare porch. She kicked off the flip-flops, crossed her legs up under her, and continued to rock and pick at her chipped, blue-painted toenails.

Detective Wilson avoided being critical, still, it was part of his job to size up people, and the smudges on her shorts appeared not to be from hard work, but rather from not being washed this year.

"Claire's been after dad's money." Sandy needed to complain and she had a listener. "She tricked dad into marriage with her. Otherwise he would have had better sense. He is weak that way. He has already been through two divorces. Women love him but soon leave because he is so arrogant and nasty. I think this pending marriage was on hold following a big argument they had." She stared at waves breaking gently down the beach. She remembered their argument and her delight about it. She picked at her toenails some more.

Detective Wilson pulled out his notebook and began entering notes. This appeared to energized Sandy to go on—reveal more vitriol about Claire.

"Claire's been giving him shots of something, too. Dad said it was vitamins, but I wonder. He was secretive about it."

"Miss Bennett, can you tell me what they argued about?"

"Oh, I don't know. I was in the next room laughing so hard . . . something Claire had done that dad didn't like."

"And you don't recall what that was?"

"Claire was always doing something that dad didn't like. Who could keep up!"

"And were you often around them?"

"No. Too unpleasant." Sandy's eyes shifted around as she realized, when she thought about it, that Claire had always tried to make their visits together pleasant, and for some reason she had hated her all the more for it. In Sandy's opinion, whatever the facts, Claire killed Tom. About thirty-five and single again for the second time, Sandy thought it would be okay for her, Sandy, to marry again, but not for her father to do so—after all he was sixty.

"Well, Miss Bennett, thank you for your help." A gross exaggeration, he thought. "Stay in town, I may have more questions as my investigation proceeds." And he carefully stepped down the rickety steps, climbed into the Mustang, made a three-point turn, and, trying not to stir up dust, proceeded down the lane. He would not be keen, he thought, to further question the Miss Sandy Bennett.

Next, Detective Wilson paid an unannounced visit to the late Tom Lewis's fiancée, Claire Johnson. Claire welcomed the detective, and politely invited him in, asking him to please take a seat. Wilson's research had established that Claire, a widow, had a part-time home business for medical billing. She was slender and tastefully put together in jeans and a crisp linen shirt, and her home seemed to smile with harmony and order. Wilson's impression was that a man could go a long way before finding a mate more pleasant than Claire. He pulled a notebook from his pocket and intended to stick to business. What had happened to Mr. Lewis was still an unknown.

"Ms Johnson, I understand that you were the person who called 911 for Tom Lewis. I've been assigned to investigate his death and need to ask you a few questions."

Claire nodded her cooperation.

"You and Tom were overheard having a heated argument. Do you recall what that was about?" he asked.

"Yes. He had begun to pick on me again . . . he wanted me to change. We did go at it. I had tried several times to stop seeing him, but he would call anyway. Our entire relationship, except for the first three months, was sour. I'm sorry about that, but not because of the money."

"What do you mean by 'the money'?"

"Well, Tom was planning to assign part of his assets to me in preparation for our upcoming marriage, but after our arguments started, he said everything would go back to his daughter, Sandy, whom he had never trusted. Since I hadn't expected anything anyway, that was fine with me."

"Strange indeed. In what way did he want you to change?"

"Petty issues. For one, he didn't like the way I speak . . . the words I use, or how I pronounce them."

"What a pest!"

"Yes. I'm from Alabama originally and I have my own diction traits . . . and words. For example, Tom became annoyed with me once because I told a man, whom we met when out for a walk, that he had a sweet little doggie. Tom said he was shocked at my word choice and I was not to use the so-called juvenile word, 'doggie.' And there were other similar instances . . . increasingly so."

"That is strange, Ms Johnson," Detective Wilson said, shaking his head in amazement. "Can you tell me something about Tom's problem with his daughter?"

"Whenever she gets money in hand," Claire said, "she bums around Europe with scragglers and never holds a job for long. For the past few years, she has demanded more money from Tom; said he owed it to her; whereas he didn't feel he owed her anything. He had paid her way through college and had given her seed money until she could find a job and get settled. Tom didn't want to enable Sandy's wasted life by supporting her."

Wilson nodded in agreement as he heard this story of conflict.

"Sandy has a degree in elementary education, but says she can't stand kids. In the jobs she has had, parents complain about her. Sandy can't stand parents either." Claire formed a tentative smile.

Detective Wilson jotted down a few impressions and turned to a clean page.

Claire used the pause to excused herself, saying she would brew coffee for them. Shortly, she returned from the kitchen with a tray set with china and cookies. She set the tray on the coffee table in front of Wilson and poured a cup for each of them. Wilson's well-dressed appearance and professional manner inspired confidence, but he noticed that, nevertheless, Claire's hands shook slightly.

"At first, I was thrilled when Tom asked me to marry him," she said. "He was one of the most interesting men I had ever met, and we had long, stimulating conversations. Tom had great curiosity and was always reading and expanding his knowledge." Her cup rattled when she sat it down, and for a few seconds she seemed lost in private flashbacks.

"What caused further blow-ups between Tom and you?" Wilson asked, looping back to his first question.

"One of the on-going problems for me was that his old girlfriends kept calling and coming by. I wanted that to stop. After all, they had broken it off, so why should it drag out and come between him and me? He had long conversations with them and led them on . . . within my hearing . . . frequently calling them 'darling'. After about the first three months I wanted to move on . . . end our relationship. It had become too hurtful and problematic."

Silence hung between them for a bit, and then Wilson said, "Ms Johnson, it's on record that you were giving Mr. Lewis injections. What did the shots contain?"

"Vitamin B12. He had asked me to give him his injections. It was only one shot every month. In addition, he went to the Bee and Balsam Naturopathic Clinic weekly for intravenous vitamin C, I think it was. He said the shots would grant him a long life span. We argued about that because I didn't want him to continue there. That place seemed full of low-lifers. I offered to connect him with a good physician instead; especially as he grew weaker by the day, but he said he had to think about it."

Claire's cat, Sophie, jumped up on her lap as if to console her.

"And finally, Tom was so weak I had to help him to the john, and to get dressed. When he had a seizure, I called 911. His house isn't far from here, just three-quarters of a mile, so it was too easy for him to give me a call to run over and help with something."

Detective Wilson didn't want to leave this pleasant woman but the job was beckoning. He thanked Claire for her time and said he had to get on with his investigation. As he backed out the Mustang, he saw her watching from her doorway.

He found the Bee and Balsam Naturopathic Clinic in a gray, one-story office building just off Route One. Inside were waiting rooms studded with artificial plants. He found himself thinking . . . natural clinic . . . unnatural plants. Taking a closer look at the plants he saw that they were all balsam with one bee attached to every leaf. In the middle was a small fountain shooting up a central jet of water. Well, he thought, they haven't invented artificial water yet. He showed his badge to the receptionist, shielded behind a window, and said he wanted to speak to Art Davies—the name Claire Johnson had given him. The receptionist used an intercom to call Art to the front.

"Please be seated, Art will be out shortly."

Wilson took a seat on a black, faux-leather couch, and sat back to wait. He studied the numerous posters, tacked up on the wall before him, that announced various natural therapies and cleansings that the clinic offered, including a fee schedule. After five minutes, Wilson saw a man approaching from down a long corridor off to the side.

"I'm Art Davies. How can I help you?" He offered the detective his hand.

Wilson introduced himself and showed Art his badge. When he explained that he had been assigned to investigate Tom Lewis's death, and wanted to determine exactly what treatment Tom had received at the clinic, Art led the detective back to a tiny examining room where they could talk privately.

"Sorry, but this is the only empty room right now," Art said.

They sat on two metal chairs the room provided. A built-in bed occupied the back wall, and drawn partially across the bed was a white curtain that tried, but didn't hide, a pile of papers and magazines stacked there. Magazines were also piled on a long table in front of where the two men sat. In an opposite corner off to the left, a computer monitor waited for instructions. The room smelled of, what Detective Wilson thought might be, massage oils.

He found Mr. Davies to be open and relaxed. About mid-thirties, Wilson thought, he appeared to keep toned and trim; reminded Wilson of a marathon cyclist.

"We were shocked to hear about Tom," Art Davies said. "His daughter called to tell us. He was an interesting man, full of life it seemed. As for his treatment, we gave him intravenously a vitamin protocol he had found on the Internet. He said it contributed to a longer, healthier life. It's not an unusual procedure and shouldn't have caused his death. The last time I saw him, he was fairly jovial, flirting with Marisa Samson, one of the other techs here. I think she was falling for him; Tom was attractive. He worked out and kept toned. Looked ten years younger than he was. Marisa always put Tom in a private room rather than in the big common room with our other clients."

Davies went on nervously, saying too much. Wilson happily let him ramble on. "Marisa and Tom caused a bit of trouble around here. I think my boss, Dr. Harry Clarke, was annoyed with them. Harry dated Marisa; considered her his property. So, when Tom arrived for his IV, Harry would hang around close by, looking sour."

There was a long pause in the room now during which Art adjusted some dials on the monitor, and wondered whether to continue that topic. Detective Wilson wrote something in his notebook as he waited. He had a way of drawing out information without uttering a word.

"I thought Tom's fiancée, Claire, was annoyed also." Art continued. "She saw how Marisa flirted with Tom, just as if Claire wasn't there. I don't know if that's the reason, but Claire stopped coming in with him, which initially she had been doing."

Detective Wilson put in a request for the crime lab to examine the clinic's waste from the last few days—look for contaminants. "Pull the waste out tonight when no one is around," he instructed his sergeant.

A fairly complicated case, he thought: Tom's daughter, Sandy Bennett, obviously hates her father; wants his money, thinks of it as her money; resents Claire Johnson. Ms Johnson gave Tom shots and had squabbles with him. The clinic owner, Dr. Harry Clarke, has issues with jealousy and perhaps Ms Johnson did as well. The finger pointed all around him. He decided another conversation with Claire Johnson might be helpful, especially about the jealousy issue. Besides, Ms Johnson was a lovely woman, and he was not adverse to conversing with lovely women.

Claire invited Detective Wilson back to her patio to enjoy the mild spring air and take in the view of her gardens while they talked. On their way through the kitchen, she poured iced-teas for them.

"It's true," Claire said, when the detective asked her about Marisa's flirtation with Tom. "Marisa was openly flirting with Tom, and he was impressed. Marisa is feminine and pretty. Most men would be taken with her. She wears frilly skirts and high-heeled sandals that show off her legs. I did notice that Dr. Clarke, the owner of the clinic, seemed to be bothered by something and hung around more. The uncomfortable situation gave me my freedom from Tom, which I had increasingly desired."

"Could you explain what you mean by your freedom?"

"It would take too long to give you the whole history, but the short version is: the first three months that Tom and I dated, he was considerate and charming. But after that nothing I did was okay with him. I think his PhD in Clinical Psychology had made him arrogant and he started letting it out. He carped on the way I spoke, as I said before, my diction, my cup of coffee in the morning, or that I did or didn't eat this or that. Controlling. For example he insisted that I should take laxatives, when in my whole life that has **not** been something I have needed." She made an ironic face. "He said he had been taking them since boyhood. Like candy; his mother had kept laxatives out in a dish. Imagine!" Claire's brain was filling with more examples crowding in. "I couldn't eat nuts around him; he was bothered by my chewing, even though I chew normally and quietly with my mouth shut," she laughed. I couldn't leave a decent tip the rare times we ate out. He wanted to leave less than ten percent, and would stare me down and utter a firm No, if I tried to put more bills on the table. I couldn't read the Sunday paper at the breakfast table. He wouldn't just be annoyed by my actions, he would yell and glare at me. There's much, much more."

"Then, forgive me for asking, and perhaps I'm out of line to ask," Wilson said, "but why did you keep seeing him?"

"Well, I certainly made the decision not to move in with him, or to marry, heaven forbid, but his increasing weakness and apparent illness made it hard to just drop him. He became less able to drive due to dizziness, and less able to cook for himself. He didn't have the strength to stand at the stove or kitchen sink that long. A small man to start, he had lost sixteen pounds. Regardless of how one felt about him . . . he needed help. His arrogance had eventually flamed off all his friends; I was the only one left."

Her frown was a good indicator of the moral struggle she had had.

"He had been kicked out of his Italian Club for misbehavior. And, when they found out he was so weak, and had nothing to offer, his former girlfriends lost interest." Claire rose and went inside for a bowl of ice and the pitcher of tea.

While she was in the kitchen, Wilson looked at her colorful garden. He felt peaceful there. He thought he could sit on this patio forever. A gentle breeze stirred about the aroma of lilies of the valley. Claire's kitty, Sophie, came out to sniff the detective's shoes and do her own investigation.

"So," Claire began, after she returned with tea and offered it to Wilson, "when Tom and Marisa started their acting out, I took that as the perfect reason to stop going in with Tom. He had caused me a good amount of stress; always judging, correcting and directing me. So, I began to stay more at home and concentrated on my business. I began to relax. Then, inevitably after a few days, he would call me to come over for dinner and to help. I knew he needed someone to cook. I couldn't say no."

After one discarded IV bag from the outside trash container at Bee and Balsam Naturopathic Clinic was found to have extremely high traces of sodium bicarbonate, Detective Wilson went back to the clinic. Once more Art Davies brought the detective back to the tiny treatment room. Then Art excused himself saying he had to check on a client and would be right back. He left the detective sitting there.

Wilson stood and looked down the hall to the right where he could see a woman lounging in a stuffed chair with an IV going into her arm. She was laughing with someone whom the detective could not see. He decided to walk to the end of the hall and take a better look. He stood in the open doorway of the large room and saw, lined up around the walls of the room, women and men outpatient clients, dressed in their street clothes, and attached to intravenous drips. They were laughing and talking loudly across the room; several with cell phones pasted to an ear. Things were scattered about here and there. A mix of stuffed chairs of various shapes, sizes, and patterns lined the walls, and an assortment of worn rugs made a half-hearted attempt to hide the scuffed and gouged floor.

How could people submit themselves to this, Detective Wilson wondered. It's too casual and disordered here—if he were they, he would worry about what was going into his veins. He had seen enough. He turned back and took his seat in the tiny room. Shortly, Art came in and asked how he could help. Wilson explained that lab results taken from the clinic's IV bags that were taken from the trash, showed that one bag had contained a high amount of sodium bicarbonate. The lab found good fingerprints on that bag and homicide techs would be in to collect fingerprints from the clinic employees.

"This could be what skewed Tom Lewis's serum pH," the detective said.

"I don't know," Art said. "That shouldn't be. I carefully check the label on each IV that I administer. A few clients are receiving a solution that contains a trace amount of bicarbonate of soda, a protocol used in Europe. It's thought to kill cancer cells, leaving normal cells intact. But not Tom Lewis; he was just receiving vitamin therapy. You might ask Harry if he knows anything about it. Harry owns this clinic and has a Ph.D. in pharmacology. He's helpful and easy going . . . thoughtful. He even gave me an extra afternoon off last week, when I mentioned that my brother was here for a visit."

Detective Wilson took notes and Art again adjusted the nearby monitor.

"Harry said he would take care of the clients who came in while I was out," Art said. "I think Tom Lewis was due to come in that afternoon, and, I think, Harry wanted to keep an eye on Marisa."

When fingerprint results came in, Detective Wilson brought Dr. Harry Clarke in to homicide for questioning. Clarke had resisted but Wilson explained that it was either come in voluntarily, or have a warrant for his arrest delivered at the clinic by police. He read Clarke the Miranda warning, and then said: "Dr. Clarke, I believe you're complicit in the death of Tom Lewis. Because of your jealousy of Marisa and her attraction to Tom, you gave him an IV containing a dangerously high solution of sodium bicarbonate. You thought it would not cause immediate death, giving you time to avoid detection. And, you judged mistakenly, that among the dozens of IV's going into your waste each day, the one you used for Tom would not be found."

Dr. Clarke looked around as though for escape. "That's impossible," he said. "I don't have time to administer the doses. I run the clinic." He slammed his fist on the table.

"But your prints were found on an IV bag in the waste container," Detective Wilson said. "That bag had extremely high, possibly lethal, traces of bicarbonate of soda. You may not actually have meant to kill Tom Lewis, but you certainly meant to weaken him and put him out of commission. You were enough afraid of losing Marisa, to take a chance on murder."

Dr. Clarke pushed forward in the stiff chair and again slammed his fist down on the table. Mouth agape, he bellowed, "Detective, go to bloody hell! Just try to prove that you have a case!"

Wilson calmly insisted: "You took your opportunity, doctor, when you gave Art Davies the afternoon off."

Finding the killer gave Detective Wilson a sense of great relief that surprised him. It was then that he realized how worried he had been about Ms Claire Johnson's possibly being implicated. Although in his clearest thinking he knew it must be impossible. How pretty she looked, he thought, as she sat petting Sophie. They lounged again on Claire's patio. Wilson had called on Claire to tell her the result of his investigation. Even though Claire had wanted to distance herself from Tom, she was owed an explanation about the cause of his death. The more they relaxed, the more Claire asked Detective Wilson about himself.

"My wife died two years ago," he said. "I haven't had time since then for much socializing. I have two grown and independent youngsters with whom I get together occasionally. That's about it."

"What led you into criminal investigation?" Claire asked.

"Actually, I have a law degree and worked as an attorney for a couple of years. But times were hard and I had only landed the job by promising the law firm that I would do surveillance and detective work for them. They provided me with a terrific mentor, a New York detective who grew up through the ranks; he taught me everything he knew. I stayed with it . . . I like the freedom. Now, I work on my own out of a home office. And I have an associate who helps me along. He gets the tough cases." Wilson laughed.

"Would you care to start some socializing right now and stay for lunch?" Claire asked. She had found the detective to be interesting and mild. Not someone who would always be correcting her.

They watched Sophie take a minute to again sniff Wilson's shoes; find out where he had been. She rubbed his cuff.

"Yes! Thank you. I'm starved," Detective Wilson said. "I think Sophie also approves."

Chef Able Kookum Goes Down

Earlier, when headquarters called, Detective Sal Marino had been having his morning coffee and thinking about his problems Now, his partner, Detective Tom Diller, and he were to go immediately to what appeared to be a homicide at the home of a famous chef, Able Kookum. The detectives had heard of him. Kookum had published two popular cookbooks and had a weekly television show.

When they arrived at the chef's home, an ambulance and an array of police cars were scattered over the lawn. And in the Kookum kitchen, smeared with a slush of chicken stock,

Chef Able Kookum lay crumpled on the tiled floor. Bits of bones, mushrooms, carrots, onions, celery, and spices lay round about and spread over his large, bulky body. Detective Marino, trying to suppress a sense of the absurd, thought the dead man looked stuffed. Off to the side lay a large cast-iron skillet that, when it landed, had cracked a piece of tile. A few bits of mushrooms still adhered to the skillet. And in the slush, a large stock pot had slid across the tiles to a far corner.

"Judging from the man's head, with the side bashed in," Detective Diller said, "I'd say that skillet is our weapon." They stood aside and observed the crime crew bagging evidence, taking photos, recording facts, and dusting for fingerprints. Medics had said there was no pulse, and judging from the wet slush on the floor in which they were trying not to slide, time of death was rather recent. The medics did not think rigor had started.

"I agree," said Diller, "Looks like a clear case of murder. Either that or assisted suicide." he gave Marino an ironic smile.

Marino hunched his shoulders and said, "Unless you can pound your own skull with 35 pounds of force, I'd agree that it's at least assisted. Perhaps not invited."

When she found Able Kookum's body, Flora Ingeborg, one of Chef Able Kookum's cooking class attendees, called 911. After the police arrived and she answered their questions, she went home greatly distressed.

Detectives Marino and Diller, with the need to acquire more information about whatever had happened to Kookum, went from the crime scene to Ingeborg's home. When she opened her front door for them, she was disarrayed and trembling, and her eyes were red and swollen. They showed her their badges, explained that they had just come from the chef's house, and wanted whatever information she could supply. She asked them to come in. "Please have a seat. I've just made coffee . . . would you have some?"

"Thank you . . . coffee will hit the spot," Marino said. Diller nodded in agreement. They sat quietly the few minutes until Flora returned with a tray bearing three cups of coffee, cream and sugar. Marino noticed that in Ms Ingeborg's hands, the tray shook slightly, rattling the cups and spoons. He took his cup, sipped the good coffee, and began his inquiry.

"Ms Ingeborg, please tell us what you found on arrival at Chef Kookum's home."

"It was horrible . . . seeing Able lying there, for all the world lifeless . . . his eyes staring up at the ceiling. I've known him a long time, you know . . . he was a good friend . . . much more than a teacher."

147

Detective Marino nodded in sympathy. He had experienced his own trauma not long ago; part of which was coming home after a grueling workday, to find that his landlady had locked him out of the house. His personal belongings were out on the grass. Not the same as a death, but still depressing. At least the landlady hadn't put out Quirky, his cat. Marino had seen Quirky through the window, looking confused. Marino had had to call the landlady to come and let him rescue Quirky.

"When you happened upon the chef lying there, did you immediately call the police from his house?" he asked Flora. Tall and solid with finely chiseled features and ears that winged out, Marino could be likened to a large, sensitive, antenna, hearing more than the interviewee was willing to tell.

Flora was fidgety. She looked as though somehow she must be in trouble. She had thought the pause to fetch coffee would give her nerves time to calm, but it hadn't helped.

"Yes," she said "My cell phone was in my pocket."

"Please tell us why you were at Mr. Kookum's home."

"At about 8:00 this morning, Able telephoned to ask whether I could come over and help make chicken stock." Her throat tightened with suppressed sobs, making it hard for her to continue. "And also help with a catering job coming up. He said he was behind today because the client had made a last minute switch from prime rib to chicken hash . . . it's the famous 'Club 21' recipe that requires stock. We were to start the stock in the morning and have our class in the afternoon, as usual." Flora's emotions swelled and she dabbed her eyes with a tissue. "About an hour later, as I was ready to leave for Able's, Emily Hosker called to say the class had been cancelled. Because of competition between us, I didn't mention to her that I would shortly be going to Able's to make stock. I figured I'd let Able do that if he had a reason to. I thought it was a bit strange though . . . that he didn't tell me he was cancelling the class." She paused to run the events through her thoughts.

"I guess when he phoned, he had not realized he was running out of time," she said. "When I knocked he didn't come to the door and so, knowing that he was expecting me, and the door was unlocked, I let myself in. When he's expecting us, he leaves the back door into the kitchen unlocked."

"Did you touch or rearrange anything while you were there?" Detective Marino asked.

"No. I couldn't bear to see Able like that. I shouted at him. He was unresponsive. I couldn't step in due to slush spread all over the slippery tile. He was lying in it. I phoned 911, and waited outside the front door until the police came. I answered their questions, gave them my address and telephone number, and told them to go in the back entrance. Then I came home to try to digest what I had just seen."

"Who else would have frequent contact with the chef?"

"Once a week, afternoons, he taught a Cordon Bleu style class for three of us: myself, Emily Hosker, and Tillie Tilson. We're all school teachers; I teach home sciences and Able's class lends itself to that. Occasionally Able would ask one of us to help him with catering jobs and sometimes we got to assist him on his weekly television show. We would tell our students to be sure and watch the show, that we would ask questions later. They loved it. You might say we were competitive to be on Able's show."

The detective recorded contact information for Emily and Tillie, closed his notebook and took a minute to consider what remained, if anything, to be said. "Technicians will have to take your fingerprints, Ms Ingeborg. It's standard procedure to fingerprint everyone who has recently been in a victim's home. It doesn't mean that you're a suspect, but you and the others will have to go down to headquarters for that. Just routine. And please stay in town in case we have further questions."

Flora assured him that would not be a problem. "But," she thought to say as she saw them off, "they will find all three sets of our prints around Able's kitchen, dining room, and in the living room where we sometimes congregated to help plan his show."

On their way to the Fishtail for lunch, Marino thought about his personal problems and what to do next. He had had to take a room at the YMCA and to put his furniture into storage, a temporary solution to his housing problem. He hoped. He had to have a home. He had too much stuff. And he had a cat. He had smuggled Quirky into his room at the Y and was afraid that any day the cleaning people would accidentally let Quirky out. He tipped them handsomely to keep quiet about Quirky and told them that shortly he would be moving Quirky. That meant he had to have a house soon, and coming up with first and last month's rent, plus security was a problem. At least he still had his car. How fortunate that he had paid off that loan.

After lunch, the detectives called on Emily Hosker. She opened the door with a glare at them that felt like a slap.

"Ms Hosker, Chef Able Kookum, your friend and mentor, has met with an accident, as you've no doubt heard by now, and we are questioning all the members of his cooking class." The detectives flipped open their badges for her to see, but her response was to reinforce her glare. This was clearly an intrusion.

"May we come in?" Marino asked. "Either that, or you will have to come down to headquarters."

Emily opened her door wider to let them enter. Speechless, she continued scowling at them. The detectives stood waiting, but she did not ask them to have a seat. Marino glanced around her living room; there were no softening touches, no color, no pictures, no pillows, no gadgets, and no curtains. Probably no kitty, Marino thought. He might as well give her the feeling that they would be here until they got whatever information she could tell, and that they expected cooperation. So he took a seat, leaned back, and studied her. Detective Diller, following Marino's example, also sat. Emily continued to stand and stare. Her wrinkled gray caftan over baggy jeans, and her hair, parted down the middle and pulled back severely, reinforced Marino's impression that self-enhancement was an unknown concept for her.

"Did you go by the chef's house this morning, Ms Hosker?" Marino asked.

Emily, now deciding that this appalling situation might last a bit, took a seat as far from the detectives as she could manage. She shifted in her chair, hesitating to answer.

"No. Flora Ingeborg, a member of our cooking class, called to tell me about the tragedy. It was hard to believe because Able had called an hour earlier, to ask me to let everyone know that today's cooking class was cancelled. He said he would need the class time to cook pies for a new catering job."

"Why would he have called you instead of one of the others?"

"Oh, mine is the first name on his list. And always has been," she added, pushing up her chin. "And he and Flora Ingeborg have been at odds lately over a cheese shredder. But I guess Flora went over there anyway."

Detective Marino saw that Emily's right hand was scarred and red across the top. "That looks like a serious burn on your hand. How did you get that?"

"I baked a pie last night and when I pulled it out of the oven I raked my hand across the rack above." She changed the subject, "How was Able killed? Or," she quickly reconsidered, "was he killed? When Flora called me about the sad news, she was in too much distress to go into it." Emily brought on a knowing squint and waited for the answer. She tried to appear her most self-possessed.

"We're not giving out details at this time, Ms Hosker, but it does look like someone attacked him. Be sure to stay around; we'll have to get your fingerprints, so please come down to police headquarters. It's just routine. And we'll probably have more questions."

Next, Marino and Diller, eager to leave Ms Hosker's cold company, called on Tillie Tilson. They hoped for a warmer reception.

Tillie had been in shock since hanging up the telephone from Flora's call. Flora couldn't tell her what had happened, just that it looked like Able had had a bad fall, appeared lifeless, was unresponsive, and she had phoned 911. Then, with ambulance and police cars all over the place, Flora said she had gone home to get out of their way and to try to absorb what she had seen.

When the detectives knocked on her door, Tillie welcomed them in. Maybe they could shed some light on this dreadful situation.

"Ms Tilson, I'm Detective Marino and this is my partner Detective Diller. We've been called to investigate Chef Able Kookum's accident." Marino was careful not to call it an attack, or possibly a murder.

"Sadly, one of my classmates has called with the ghastly news," Tillie said. "How is Able? Did he make it?"

"I'm afraid not, Ms Tilson."

"Oh no!" Her face twisted with emotion. "What happened to him?"

"We're not certain; perhaps you can help us. We need to know something about him and about anyone with whom he associated. How did Chef Kookum treat everyone? Was he well liked? Do you know of any enemies he may have had? . . . that kind of information. We've already spoken to Ms Ingeborg and Ms Hosker, and we'd like to hear what you can add."

"He had no enemies that I was aware of, and he was definitely well liked," Tillie said. "There was always a waiting list for his classes, and he would take only three students at a time. The only students of his I know are Flora and Emily in my class."

Detective Marino wrote in his notebook and waited for more.

Tillie had to make an effort to stay composed as she continued, "And, we all wanted to be his assistant . . . it was an honor. His cuisine was renowned. And, although it was nerve wracking, I loved it when he asked me to be his assistant on his show. I teach school . . . third grade . . . and the youngsters get a kick out of seeing me on TV."

Detective Marino could see that Tillie would be a beautiful addition to the chef's show. A pretty and slender woman, she was poised and well-spoken. A clingy white knit top clung to her just right, and a soft blue skirt showed off toned legs. On her feet were jeweled sandals. To Marino she seemed clever, and also feminine.

"Did you see him this morning?" He tried not to look her over, but he was thinking how nice it would be for her to cook for him.

"Actually, I did," Tillie said. "Quite early . . . it must have been around 8:30 . . . I drove over to borrow the cheese shredder. It's Flora's invention and Able had the only prototype. Last week Flora asked me to try it out and let her know what I thought, and I had not yet had a chance to do that. I didn't go in because the door was locked, and when I knocked, and Able opened it, he acted rushed." Tillie wonder what else she might know that would be important. "Before I knocked, I thought I heard raised voices, but it could have been the television or radio. There were no cars in his driveway, and he acted as though he was alone . . . just in a rush to get on with the cooking. Now I wonder who was there. When Flora called me later to tell me the horrible news, she said that Able had asked her over to help make stock, and she had found him unresponsive on the floor."

"Can I get you something to drink?" she asked.

Both detectives declined. They had just stopped for a quick hamburger and it was getting late. They still had to file reports back at headquarters. Marino thought how he would like to have a drink with her some other time; that would brighten up his bad days of late, but he didn't say it—that would be out of line. Stick to business.

A faint "mew" sounded from around the corner of the living room.

"That's a familiar sound," Marino said.

"That's Chatter, my cat. She's quite vocal. It takes her a little time to come out when guests are here. Come on Chatter. Come say hello."

Chatter appeared and cautiously stationed herself in the doorway, ears alert. Marino said hello to Chatter. He said that he liked cats and had one at home—which temporarily was one room at the Y.M.C.A. He added that Quirky, his cat, didn't like living in one room. Chatter approached the detective, and by way of sympathy, sniffed his shoes.

"Chatter, can you think of anything else that might help us solve this case?" Marino asked.

Tillie managed an awkward smile; this was not a time for joking. "I don't think Chatter can help . . . she has never met Able." Tillie arranged her skirt and continued to think about what happened at Able's house when she went for the cheese shredder. "Able didn't ask me in, but he said he needed the shredder and I could have it later. It's strange that he didn't mention cancelling class. But as I said, he seemed to be in a rush." Her expression clouded over. "That reminds me of something that could be important. During our last class I overheard Able and Flora arguing. Apparently, if Flora didn't agree to his percentage, Able might manufacture the shredder without her permission. She didn't sound happy. I can't imagine that he would do that, but there it is."

Aside from Chef Able Kookum's needless and unexpected catastrophe, what had occurred to impact Tillie was that Able's death, if indeed he were dead, would be the end of his cooking classes. Joining his classes had been a light and creative way to be involved in something, and make new friends. Tillie had thrived in Able's class, and often he had asked her to help with catering for a private party. And increasingly he asked her to assist on his television show. Both of those activities brought in the extra income that she needed, and colored her days brighter, less gray.

The brooding over her divorce last year and the crush of rejection by her husband, Barry's, leaving her for a younger woman, was growing fainter with each week. She had never wanted her marriage to end. She had flowered in the marriage without suspecting that Barry was involved with someone he met on the Internet. Tillie had had no way to sense that he was restive, and could be pulled away from her so easily. And the constant adjustment to wake each day and realize once again that she was alone. Yes, she had a classroom full of cute youngsters at the school where she taught third grade, but that was not the same. Chef Able had become a friend—and now this. For many reasons this would be a tragic loss.

Before going home for the night, the detectives stopped off at Waters Edge for a beer, and to talk over what they had learned from the investigation. "How are you holding up?" Diller asked. It's been a year now since your wife died. Is it getting any better?"

"I've had some problems, mostly with finances. You couldn't imagine how five years of her illness and all those hospitalizations and prescriptions depleted our savings. The bills are still coming in. One bill alone for twenty-four hours at Duke: fifty thousand. Of course I have insurance, but that covers only eighty percent, and often much less. And so many bills come in, you wonder whether they're all legit."

"Damn, how do you do it," Diller asked.

"I don't. I lost the house I was renting. That's why I'm living at the Y. If only the landlord had been willing to wait one more month . . . I sold some stuff and would have been able to pay her. However, I'm working down the bills, and soon I'll be able to rent a cottage. Quirky doesn't want to live in one room forever. Basically, all we need as we go through life is a mate, a cottage, a small garden, and a cat," he laughed. "That's all! Therefore, when Quirky and I find the cottage, I'll put in a small garden. Then I'll have three out of four. That ain't half bad. It's lonely though."

"Best thing to do is get involved in something outside of work, but with our schedules that's hard to do," Detective Diller said.

The next morning the detectives studied photographs, notes, and lab reports spread before them across a conference table. Clearly, the head wound was the cause of death, and the cast-iron skillet was deemed the weapon. The body had signs of scalding, so the chef must have been carrying the huge pot of hot liquid when struck by the skillet. Adhering to the skillet were pieces of blood and flesh. However, due to being awash in the large quantity of chicken stock flooding the floor, no fingerprints were available on the skillet. Elsewhere there was an abundance of fingerprints from all three class members and from Chef Kookum.

"We are missing information, and right now there are no clues," Detective Marino said. "This afternoon while we're waiting for phone records, which might tell us something, we'll fingerprint the three women, and assemble them together for further questioning. See how they interact. More might come out inadvertently; someone may trip up."

Detective Diller placed his recorder in the middle of the table and turned it on. For the record, he stated the date, time, names of the attending detectives, and the names of the three women seated before him. He stated that the women had been members of the victim's, cooking class.

Even though the recorder would be taking down the audio, Detective Marino drew out his notebook and opened it to a blank page. He leaned back in his chair and studied the three women: Flora Ingeborg, Emily Hosker, and Tillie Tilson. He had poured coffee around to help put them at ease and to occupy their nervous hands. Cream, sugar, and spoons had been set about. Cups and saucers rattled on the table. He cleared his throat and started the interrogation by asking: "How did Chef Able Kookum treat everyone? Was he well liked?"

"Yes, absolutely," the women agreed, heads nodding.

He had asked this question of the three women before, but now that some time had passed, this was a fresh start, and he might receive different answers. He wrote something, and then looked up at the three women. "Let's review what happened yesterday . . . who saw Chef Kookum, and who did not. Miss

Ingeborg, please start," he said, nodding to Flora.

"Able called me early yesterday, about 8:00, to ask if I could come over to help make chicken stock. The museum had made a last minute menu change from rib roast to chicken hash . . . the famous 'Club 21' recipe. The dinner was to be a large fund-raising event, and that volume of hash would require a lot of stock. In the past, when we cooked up this dish, not only did we use stock in the sauce, but also the chicken was initially poached in stock, and of course, Able always made fresh stock."

Flora was urged on by Marino's reassuring nods.

"He had also asked me to help with catering, which would have been tomorrow. I've called the museum, and without going into details, I told them Mr. Kookum would not be able to do the job, and to find another caterer. I gave them the name of a good replacement."

"I wondered why he was making chicken stock," Emily Hosker interrupted. "He told us last week that the museum had ordered prime rib. I was surprised he hadn't called me to help."

Marino gave her a look.

She pulled a pout. "I just live a block from him . . . he and I've been friends for years. He usually calls me. My specialty is pastry, especially pâté brisee. Able always wanted me to make the quiches." She seemed unable to stop talking, and Detective Marino noticed that she liked to play with her bracelet clasp, as though nothing else was on her mind.

Flora pursed her lips, set her cup down rather hard and butt in. "True, but lately he hired me."

"Ms Ingeborg, please continue describing the condition in which you found the chef," Marino said.

Painful though it was, Flora once more relived what she had seen when she stepped into Chef Able's kitchen. Again, Detective Marino watched the women's reaction as they absorbed Flora's graphic portrayal.

"Ms Hosker, I've asked you this before, but now we want your answer for the record, did you go by the chef's house this morning?"

Emily avoided Marino's penetrating gaze. She shifted in her chair and thought about her answer. "No, but I waited by the phone in case he called me to help make pies. As I've already told you, he did call to ask me to let Flora and Tillie know that our afternoon class was cancelled, which I did."

"I believe you said earlier that he needed the time to bake pies. But he didn't appear to be making pies," Marino said.

"It was to be his afternoon task." Emily tightened her teeth together as though finally, that's all she had to say about any of it.

"He didn't mention pies to me," Flora interjected. "He just said stock."

Marino again noticed Emily's deeply burned hand. "Ms Hosker, how was it that you burned your hand? . . . I've forgotten."

"I baked a pie night-before-last and, pulling it out of the oven, I raked my hand across the hot rack above."

Flora and Tillie turned to stare at her; Emily wasn't known to do any cooking for herself.

Detective Marino stood. "Take a break for a few minutes and stretch. I'll get water for everyone. If you want to use the facilities . . . down the hall, first door on the right." After stating the time and the break, Detective Diller stopped the recorder.

When Detectives Marino and Diller came back into the room, they passed around bottles of water, and then took their seats across from the women. Diller started the recorder. "All right," Marino said, "lets' try to finish this. I have only a few more questions. Ms Ingeborg, we've heard that you invented a fancy cheese shredder."

"Yes." Her face brightened with a smile. "It makes swirls . . . larger ones than the shredders on the market now, and also, it works nicely on cold butter: nice to shred over a casserole before putting it into the oven." Her sad eyes brightened just a bit and focused on Marino.

"Able loved it. He was going to demonstrate it on his show."

"We've heard that there was a problem between you and the chef about marketing the shredder. Please tell us about that," Marino said.

"After I patented it and had the prototype manufactured, Able wanted to market it. That would have been quite natural, considering his popular TV show. We did not agree on percentages though. I was out major expenses getting to that stage of product development. I needed a healthy percentage of the sales to recoup some of that. Able could have plugged the shredder during his show with little or no additional expense. We argued when I pointed that out to him."

"Is it true that the chef was threatening to manufacture the shredder without your permission?" Marino ventured a guess.

To drive home her point, Flora pounded her water bottle on the table. "Able would never have done that. It was just a matter of percentages, and we would have worked that out." She appeared to be blocked, unable to go on, but she heaved a sigh, and pulled in a resolve to continue. "I still can't believe how I found him . . . stock and soup bones spilled all over the floor with him lifeless in the middle." Tears formed in her eyes, and she nervously wadded her tissue and dabbed her face. She thought if she could bring back Able, she would give him the rights to the shredder outright. "Originally, in the afternoon class, we were to butterfly and stuff pork tenderloin." The corners of her mouth stretched lower. "Of course, that's unimportant now."

Detective Marino, bored now with this interrogation, drew in a long impatient breath. He tapped his pen on the table a few times, and then wrote something in his notebook. The women, nerves frayed, looked around, straining to find some diverting interest in the features of the featureless room.

Finally, Marino said, "Ms Hosker you said Chef Able Kookum called you to let the others know that the afternoon class was cancelled."

"Yes."

"And you did not go to his house."

"No." I did not," she nattered on. "He did not ask me to help, and class was cancelled, so there was no reason to go over."

"Ms Hosker, I want you to stay for further questioning. Ms Ingeborg and Ms Tilson, you may leave."

On Detective Marino's part of the globe, the spring day appeared more clear and warm than usual, with forsythia budding out all over. As he drove to Tilly Tilson's home, Marino was feeling pretty cheerful. He had told Quirky that he would say hello to Chatter for him.

Tillie answered her door with a smile and invited Marino in. She had seen through the side glass panel that it was he, right on time. He had called to ask if she would be home at 9:00 a.m., as he had some information. She agreed she would be there, and 9:00 o'clock was fine. She had coffee ready. She couldn't imagine what he had to say, but knew that she hadn't been in Able's house the day he was killed. Moreover, she had found Detective Marino to be an appealing man. She asked him to have a seat and she would serve coffee. Meanwhile, Marino was amused to see Chatter coming to greet him and once again to sniff his shoes. From the detective's shoes, Chatter knew all about Quirky.

"You're a nice cat," Marino said. "I can tell by this tidy room that you don't scratch the furniture."

"Oh, no," Tillie said, as she came into the room carrying a silver tray, on which was china, coffee, cream and sugar, and half a blueberry coffeecake. "She has a scratching post, and she gives it a good workout."

Marino's eyes lit up at the sight of the coffeecake, and he took a large slice. "My cat, Quirky, is unhappily deprived at present. He's confined to one room and gets restive, but still he doesn't scratch the furniture. Anyway, my furniture is in storage and I'll be renting a cottage shortly, one where Quirky can go out. I told him that, and he said 'hurry up.' " They laughed at their shared humor. Marino treated his coffee with cream and stirred it, thinking how best to say what he had to say next. Tillie waited, giving him space to think. Judging from the way Marino's smile had retreated—changed now for a serious face—what he had to say next might be awful. Even Chatter stood statue-like and waited.

"The bad news, Ms Tilson, is that Ms Emily Hosker has confessed to striking Chef Able Kookum with the cast-iron skillet. That blow killed him. We do not believe that she meant to kill him, but she said that she yanked the heavy iron pan off the chef's stove, and in a rage, struck him down. Her hand was scalded when he dropped that huge pot filled with near-boiling stock, which went all over the place."

"Oh, my . . . ." Tillie did not know what else to say. She had not guessed that the attacker had been one of the other class members.

"Moreover," Marino continued, "Ms Hosker said she was angry because the chef was more frequently asking you and Ms Ingeborg to assist him with catering, as well as to appear on his show. And not only did it mean a loss of income, but the school children had begun judging you three teachers according to who was on the show. So, she had walked over to have it out with him."

Knowing his news was painful, he stopped for a moment to seek the best words. "First, her burned hand, an important clue staring us in the face, seemed significant somehow. Then she tripped up during our group meeting when she said that she had wondered why the chef was making stock. Had she not been at his house that morning, she likely would not have known about the stock. Then there was the pie she said she had made that she couldn't produce. When we asked her for a small sample, she said it had failed and she had put it down the disposal. And finally, Able's telephone records show that he had no intention to cancel class. He had not phoned her."

He paused to pet Chatter. Tillie took the opportunity to freshen their coffee. She could barely grasp what the detective had to say. She knew that Able had met with a terrible fate, but to think that someone she knew had caused it!

Marino sipped his coffee, and continued explaining. "After her rage, she walked home, just a block away, and called you and Ms Ingeborg to say that class was cancelled, that the chef had ask her to call you. She did not want either of you to go over there. She did not know that Ms Ingeborg would go over anyway because he had earlier asked her to help make stock."

They sipped coffee, letting the silence massage the information the detective had just disclosed.

"I shudder at the thought that perhaps, when I knocked on Able's door to borrow the shredder, Emily might have been there," Tillie said. "I thought I heard raised voices, but, as I said earlier, it could have been a television or radio. He did seem stressed, and said he would let me have the shredder later. He didn't ask me to come in, which was odd. If he had asked me in, and Emily was there, maybe she would have calmed down, and he wouldn't have been killed. Or, if he hadn't answered the door, and if it had not been locked, I would have opened it and peeked in . . . that was our custom . . . and what would I have found?"

"Well, that we cannot know," Marino said.

This awful news took some digesting and Tillie sat quietly drinking her coffee, watching Marino pet Chatter. Then she had a thought on a lighter note.

"Detective Marino, why not bring Quirky over here until you get moved. I know that Chatter likes other cats. Maybe Quirky does also. At least it's worth a try. And, I have a high fence in the back yard from which cats can't escape. I'm sure Quirky will be safe here."

Marino, normally used to anything that came down, was thrown off guard by Tillie's kind suggestion, and nearly dropped his cup.

"I think Quirky might welcome that change. Thank you," he said, after he collected his wits. "But Quirky would insist that we had to know you better before he would submit to the transfer, and I think we might start by asking if you will have dinner with me. Tonight, if you can arrange that. And please call me, 'Sal.'"

As Detective Marino pulled out of Tillie's driveway, a feeling he had not had in a long time, found its way into his soul. He had forgotten that things change. Maybe after all he was born with some lucky genes. The big event today was that he would be taking Tillie Tilson, whom he greatly admired, to dinner. Quirky would have to agree, by cracky. Strange to think that a murder could have a positive outcome.

A Murder at Canyon Grove
Retirement Residence

"Now why'd Mr. T go and get hisself killed?" It was a rhetorical question from the grieving handyman, Joel Greaves. "Law, I can't believe this. And him such a nice man. Him and me was friends. Mr. Townsend paid me handsome to hep him wit his kitty. Now what's gonna happ'n to Willie?"

That is how a story begins that I heard while living in the desert town of Green Valley, Arizona. Many times I've been asked about this, thus I'm putting it down for the record.

Joel sat in the Canyon Grove Retirement Residence reception kiosk, hat in hand, commiserating with the day receptionist, Hannah Baker, while she sorted mail into four piles for the four different wings of the large residence facility. Hannah and Joel were horrified by the suggestion that the late Mr. Raymond Townsend, familiarly known as "Mr. T," may have been poisoned. The police were down in Mr. T's apartment working on the case now. A tragic event.

Nevertheless work had to go on; all the other residents' needs had to be taken care of, and an effort was being made to keep the unfortunate situation quiet. When questioned by curious residents, Joel and Hannah tried to act as though nothing important had happened. Detective Gus Estrada and his associate, Detective Mike Collins, had just been shown the way to Mr. Townsend's apartment.

Joel held Willie in his lap as Hannah and he quietly discussed the situation.

"Mr. T was 84 and known to have a heart condition . . . why do they suspect poisoning?" Joel asked.

Mr. Townsend had been a special friend to Joel, often inviting him to come along as his guest when the activity director took a group of residents in the van for pizza, or to a local bistro. Something different.

"I heard it was the way you found him," Hannah said. "They think his death was unnatural because something caused him to have a seizure. Steve asked me to tell you that when the police and detectives finish in Mr. T's room, to put Willie back in there until we're given further instructions. And please continue to care for him as you have."

Joel looked down at the cat curled up and purring in his lap. "I'm sorry for you, Mr. Willie," he said as he stroked the animal. "I don't know what'll happen to you now. If they let me take you home, I'll share wit you. But, it'll be slim pickin' witout that extra money Mr. T gave me to hep him."

Willie said "burrrup." He didn't know where Mr. T was, but he knew Joel was his friend. And for now that was just fine.

Waiting for a burrito to baked, Detective Gus Estrada nursed his ritual morning cup of coffee, black and strong. The chilly fall day promised to be beautiful with sun just now pushing over the mountains. Clouds should form later in the day, and Estrada hoped for rain; in this desert terrain, rain was always a blessing. As he waited, he assessed the path his life was taking, and wished his life could change color like the mountain shadows gliding over the moving earth.

Before he could think ahead and plan his day, the call came. He turned off the oven and scarfed down half the burrito; let the rest wait. He put on his pistol holster and started over to Canyon Grove Retirement Residence. Headquarters had said the death of one of the residents there appeared to be unnatural. As he drove the seven miles to the residence, he continued to estimate where he should be in his life by now. Professionally, things were okay. His social life was dismal.

When his first wife, Mary, died, he had thought life was really over. Then he met Gloria and life looked wonderful—at least for three years—until she said she had met someone else and wanted a divorce. So, one widowhood and one divorce, and now living alone. He didn't like that much. He hadn't realized that he was the only one who had enjoyed the meals Gloria and he had together. Maybe he cooked spaghetti too often. He tried to vary it, sometimes putting in coins of grilled kielbasa, and other times sautéed mushrooms, and sometimes both. He should have tried to be more imaginative. Gloria hadn't cooked much, wanted to be waited on, especially when she came in late. Shopping, she said, and doing research at the library for the book she planned.

Now days Detective Estrada hoped he never had to retire, for the work gave him something for which to live. And, he was good at his career. Was lucky to have Detective Mike Collins for his partner.

When Estrada arrived at Canyon Grove, Detective Collins was waiting for him. The residence manager, Steve Lopez, showed them to the deceased's apartment.

"Gus, we found Mr. Townsend frozen in this bizarre position," the police captain in charge said. "He must have been in the throes of a seizure."

Technicians were dusting for fingerprints, and a police photographer worked around the scene photographing Mr. Townsend. His body had tightened into a twisted, curled position over a breakfast table next to a window overlooking the inner courtyard. As they studied the apartment, both detectives jotted down notes, and watched the crime crew bagging any items that might prove to be evidence. Police were coming and going through the apartment's main entry that opened into an internal hallway. The circular hallway led east to the front reception kiosk and main entrance, and led west around in a loop to the library, kitchen, and dining room.

Curious and excited residents had gathered in the hallway to gossip about this horrid event. Someone had overheard the words, *unnatural death*. The deceased's next-door neighbor,

Maggie Smith, appeared to be entertaining them as they all stood a safe distance away.

"Apparently, this morning, when he went in to take care of Willie, Joel found Ray dead," Maggie said. "I heard Joel knock several times on Ray's door. Then I didn't hear anything for a few seconds. Then I heard Ray's telephone ring. That must have been Joel phoning him, for soon, when I put out my laundry for service, I saw Joel using his key to enter the apartment. The police and Steve arrived about fifteen minutes later."

Suddenly Maggie Smith felt some of the importance due to her. Too bad that it took the death of her neighbor to give her that feeling. She had felt insignificant for so many years, although she had carried around fame of sorts, having played stand-in for Betty Davis in Hollywood; a career about which she often reminded anyone who would listen. At age ninety, one gets little attention, even in this home of many aged people. Now, she was a fount of information, and some who lived along that hallway, and had heard the commotion, came to her with questions. One of them invited Maggie in for coffee—that hadn't happened before.

As they waited for any information that forensics could provide, the detectives started their round of questions with Steve Lopez. They took seats in Steve's office. Though he had done nothing untoward, Steve felt guilty pressure, and needing something to provide a distraction, he asked the receptionist, Hannah, to put on a pot of coffee.

"The people who may have had contact yesterday with Mr. T," Steve started, "are the front desk receptionists, and our wait-staff in the dining room. Mr. T usually eats three meals there. And I think his nephew, Oliver Townsend, came to visit him yesterday. I could check the front desk sign-in sheet to verify that. Usually Oliver visits twice a week after he closes his flower shop for the day.

"In addition, we have numerous caregivers on duty around the clock and a nurse attending during the day. She dispenses medications for those of our residents who need help with that. We also have a security guard on duty from 11:00 p.m. to 7:00 a.m. Every hour, he checks door locks, various public rooms such as the library, lounges, and dining room, and all hallways throughout the building. The residence is laid out into a four-leaf clover with interior hallways circling around each leaf, as it were. And every apartment has two exits: one into the inner hallway, the other into the large, inner courtyard, or to the outside." He jerked a paperweight around on his desk as if to demonstrate. "There are other employees for laundry, cleaning, maintenance, driving, and activities. About forty-five people, some full-time, some part-time. So I cannot, of course, know exactly whom Mr. Townsend encountered."

Hannah came in with a tray of coffee for the three men. This was not part of her job, and she shouldn't be leaving reception, but this was an extreme situation and she would pitch in and help where she could. She poured coffee into mugs that were printed with the words, "Age is the rage at Canyon Grove."

A tiny bit chunky but proportioned just right, and with shiny, brown curls circling an intelligent face, Ms Hannah Baker could be his personal receptionist any day, Detective Estrada thought. When she left with the tray, he tried not to be obvious observing her fine legs in that slinky skirt. About his age, he thought; looked to be mid-thirties, and he was forty. Well, stick to work—she was probably spoken for.

"I don't think Mr. T would have contact with the security guard, unless he had been out roaming the hallways during the night," Steve said. "That does happen, though. Sometimes residents are just restless and want to walk . . . at any hour. As for contact with a caregiver, if a resident calls for help, a caregiver goes to that room, and afterward records the incident in a log. I review that log each morning. Last night Mr. T did not call for a caregiver."

Steve opened a computer file from which he printed a list with employee telephone numbers, addresses, and work schedules. He marked the ones who might have had contact with Mr. Townsend. He also gave the detectives the telephone number of Mr. Townsend's nephew, Oliver Townsend, and told them where to find his flower shop. As he talked, Steve fidgeted and stirred his coffee too often, always dropping his spoon with a clank on the bare wood of his desk. Although their mugs were nearly full, every five minutes Steve would jump up and pour another round of coffee.

Meanwhile Detective Collins recorded his impressions in a small notebook.

"There's also Joel Greaves one of our handymen," Steve said. "Joel has only one hand . . . highly unemployable, but Mr. T asked us to take him on, and he *is* handy. Did a lot for Mr. T and Mr. T paid him for his services. Joel took care of Mr. T's cat and did other chores for him, as well as some around our facility. Mr. T gave Joel a key to his apartment. Joel has had more contact with Mr. T than any of us."

"What will happen to Mr. Townsend's cat now?" Estrada asked.

"I don't know. We'll have to work that out. Perhaps his nephew will take it."

"Have there been any problems related to Mr. Townsend? Conflicts he had with anyone?" Estrada asked.

"Well . . . ."

The detectives sipped coffee and waited.

"I can't think of anything. Mr. T had no enemies that I know of. He was kind to everyone and respected by all. His nephew, Oliver Townsend, came to visit him regularly, often taking him out for dinner. They seemed to get along fine. Although . . . ," Steve paused, "the last time they came in from dinner, I thought both of them looked angry; closed-mouth and snippy. Oliver always pushes Mr. T's wheelchair through our double doors, and normally they come in laughing about something. This time they were glum."

This was pure invention. Steve was feeling the heat and wanted to detour the detectives in a different direction. He rocked his chair back, propping his foot on the large, bottom, desk drawer that he had pulled out. Twirling his pen, he paused to watch Collins taking notes.

"I don't know what was wrong. Oliver pushed Mr. T down to his room, and I saw them no more that evening. I usually leave for home between 5:00 and 6:00, so I was probably gone when Oliver left."

Detective Estrada observed that from behind his desk, Steve could see out into the lobby and could see whoever came and went.

He noticed that Steve kept checking his watch. Detective Collins saw Steve motion to someone. He would stake his dinner on a polecat if Steve hadn't subtly nodded *no*. Collins was reluctant to be obvious and turn to see who it was, but murder was murder. He turned his head and saw two women in the reception kiosk, plainly visible from Steve's office. Neither of the women looked at Collins, and when he turned back around to face Steve—Steve gave him a blank look.

"Why do you have two receptionists now?" Collins asked.

"The shift is changing," Steve said. "Hannah leaves now, and Mercedes Salinas starts her shift. Hannah has to fill in Mercedes about anything of significance that has happened on her shift."

Detective Estrada noted the time and saw that it was 3:00 p.m. He turned and looked back at reception and saw Mercedes staring at Steve. Estrada tried not to be distracted, but the receptionist, Hannah, with pretty legs, who had served them coffee, was just leaving.

After satisfying their need for preliminary information, the detectives left, planning to continue the investigation the next day. Estrada would question any Canyon Grove employees whom they had missed, and Collins would follow up with the forensics regarding evidence taken. Headquarters had already begun to trace phone calls to and from Mr. Townsend's line. And technicians were scheduled to come to Canyon Grove and fingerprint all individuals most likely to have had contact with Mr. Townsend.

But first, Estrada and Collins agreed to drop into the Elks Lodge for a beer to top off the night. The Elks Lodge was one of few places for entertainment in this small town, and they could count on a decent time there evenings, watching people on the dance floor. One beer for Collins because his wife would be cooking dinner. Estrada, with no one waiting at home, had a second. They compared notes about the day and who at Canyon Grove might be guilty. It definitely looked as though Mr. Townsend's death was assisted. Collins told Estrada about the communication he witnessed between the manager and someone. Who? He couldn't say, but when he looked around he saw two women in reception. It looked suspiciously as though Steve had been signaling *no* to them, or at least to one of them. Estrada said he had caught that look as well and wondered.

At home, Detective Estrada started ground beef for spaghetti. Not ordinary ground beef, he had stopped by his favorite butcher on Duval Mine Road, and had had some chuck specially ground for him. He put filtered water on to boil for the pasta, and started a Sibelius CD. Was it worthwhile cooking for one? He thought so, but not necessarily every night, and he would often plan a dish with leftovers for the next night's dinner. As he relaxed over his meal, he reviewed the facts surrounding Mr. Townsend. Until forensics supplied their report, there wasn't much to go on. It was unfortunate that the case involved a death, for it definitely had energized him and would sharpen his skills. He looked forward to the next day.

Wednesday morning, Detective Collins agreed that he should wait at headquarters to follow up with forensics, and as well, obtain the warrants needed for Mr. Townsend's mail, phone, and bank records. If Townsend had indeed been poisoned, as it appeared, all kinds of possible reasons came to mind for a killer's revenge. And they had to trace every one.

Detective Estrada started his investigation by asking to be let into Mr. T's apartment. Except for the crime techs removing a cup with cocoa remains, and certain other items to take to the lab, nothing appeared to have been touched. With gloves on, Estrada pulled open drawers and closets. Clothing hung in an organized manner, and shelves of files were neatly stacked. From a drawer he removed a half dozen letters and sat in Mr. Townsend's easy chair to read clues they might contain.

Willie, who patiently had been observing this invasion of his patron's privacy, let out a sharp meow as he stared at Estrada.

"Don't worry, Willie, I won't hurt anything," Estrada said, calming the kitty.

One of the letters started out innocently enough: "Hope you are well," that stuff, but in the second paragraph the letter became wildly interesting. It read:

> If you don't legally recognize me as your natural offspring, I'm prepared to get a court ordered DNA test. One way or another I intend to be eligible under your will, or I'll sue your estate. My mother suffered long enough because of you, and I'm doing something about it in her name.

The letter was unsigned. Who? What? Estrada wondered. There was no letterhead or envelope to identify the writer. He laid the letter aside and opened the next one, which was a copy of Mr. Townsend's reply, and read:

> You are quite mistaken and misguided. I have never had children. Your late mother

was a respected member of
our household staff, and she
and I had almost no contact.
My late wife dealt with the
staff. You are welcome to all
the DNA testing you wish.

This letter-copy bore a recent date, Estrada
noted. He put the letters into an evidence bag to
be checked for fingerprints; he would need a
warrant for them. He dialed Collins and
specified the warrant he wanted. As he was
leaving Mr. T's apartment, Maggie Smith came
out of her door. From the printout that Steve
Lopez had provided, Estrada had already
established who Mr. Townsend's neighbors
were.

"Ah, I'm pleased to meet you, Ms Smith.
I'm Detective Estrada." He showed her his
badge. "I would like an hour of your time for a
few questions."

Maggie fluttered her eyelashes at Estrada
and stepped back in a pose, one hand on her
hip, the other hand tucking her cane across the
other hip. "Indeed," she said. She was glad to
be asked; she had much to tell. She stepped
back into her apartment and invited him in. She
asked him to have a seat, and with a great flurry
of scarves and skirt, she took a seat close to
him.

When he scanned the array of photos that she had arranged on a side table, she said, "That's me as Betty Davis. I was her stand in."

"I see." He wasn't going to let her distract him. "Ms Smith, have you heard anything unusual from Mr. Townsend's apartment?"

"Not only have I heard, but I have seen." She rolled her eyes.

Estrada drew out his notebook and pen. "Which came first, Ms Smith?"

"Please call me Maggie."

She had to be in her nineties, the detective thought. Curly blond hair; perfectly smooth face—a lot of work done there, he thought, but extremely wrinkled hands, arms, and neck, revealing her years. The more flirtatious she sounded; the cooler was Estrada's demeanor.

"Mornings and nights I sometimes see Joel, the handyman. He cares for Willie, Ray's cat . . . I call Mr. Townsend 'Ray'. Joel has his own key. Sometimes I hear Ray and Joel talking. These walls could be thicker, you know." She gave Estrada a beguiling smile. It was a long-practiced smile, the detective thought—the kind he had long practiced avoiding.

"Go on . . . I know about Joel and Willie."

"Well . . . I've also seen both of the day receptionists going and coming. Both Hannah, who is here days, and Mercedes, who is here evenings. For all I know they're helping with something." More rolling eyes. "As for what

I've heard . . . raised voices one evening. I quickly turned down my TV to hear what was being said, but was too late. I heard Ray's door slam. I looked out, but these stiff joints take a minute to get going, and whoever it was got around the curve of the hallway before I could see. Once I saw Mercedes, the night receptionist, going in rather late . . . I thought that was strange. I had just opened my door to pick up the weekly menu from the dining room . . . they leave one on each landing." Maggie vigorously tapped her cane and continued. "I heard Ray and Joel come in later, so I knew Ray had not been home when Mercedes went in, and I knew Joel, not Mercedes, was taking care of Willie. So, as I said, that was rather strange."

"Did you mention this to Mr. Townsend?"

"No, I try to mind my own business." She swapped her smile for a smug look.

That would amaze me, thought Detective Estrada.

On his way in his regulation new Ford sedan to talk to Joel, Estrada thought about what a strange town this was; actually, he thought this often: a dry oasis ringed with copper mines, golf courses, and dust. And, let's not leave out valley-fever. A golf and bridge mindset. Lily white. Not a likely place for a half-black man with one hand to find work. He wondered how Joel came to be here.

Joel lived in a mobile home down West Calle Dos, a county road about a half-mile from a town road; not the easiest location to find. A dirt road, or rather sand—no dirt here. An area to be shared with coyotes, wild cats, Javelenas, giant owls, turkey buzzards, snakes, and scorpions. Plenty of those, Estrada imagined. He pulled into Joel's driveway and stepped out of the dust-covered car. Joel was expecting him. Mr. Townsend had given Joel a prepaid mobile phone and always made sure the phone had minutes. He hadn't wanted Joel to be alone in the desert without a phone.

Detective Estrada looked around at the well-cared-for grounds. Two palo verdes bordering the singlewide mobile home provided relief from the sun, and Texas Rangers had recently dropped their blossoms, spreading an orchid carpet around. The sandy yard was raked clean in an attempt to make Zen-like patterns. Apparently, one hand could perform as well as, or better than, two.

Joel was waiting at the door and welcomed Estrada.

"How are you doing, Joel?" Estrada asked, shaking Joel's hand. Joel replied that he was doing as well as could be expected. He offered the detective a tall glass of iced tea and they took seats inside in the clean and orderly sitting area. Joel was relaxed. He understood that, though he might be considered a person of interest in the strange death of Mr. T, many other Canyon Grove employees were as well.

"I spoke to Steve and, Joel . . . it's uncertain that they'll keep you on now."

"Yes, sir," Joel said. "Hannah told me she overheard I might be let go. She said she would hep me find somethin' else, if I was."

"Joel, I have to ask everyone these questions."

"Yes, sir."

"Please call me Gus. All my friends call me Gus. And drop the 'sir.'"

"Yes, sir."

"When did you last see Mr. Townsend alive, and what was the occasion?"

"Tuesday. Mr. T took me to dinner at the casino wit a group from the res'dence. Often the activity director takes a group out in the van. Sometimes we go to the casino for the buffet, because some like to push a few coins into the bandits. Mr. T does. Since I hep him wit his chair, he always insists on buyin' me dinner, and gives me a sawbuck to feed a machine. That's all he risks hisself. Him and me usually lose that right away. Mr. T just laughs. 'Price of an evening out,' he would always say. Then I would wheel him around to look at all the people and machines until the van was ready to leave."

Estrada could see the affection and the loss Joel felt.

"Mr. T could walk jes fine . . . he only used the wheelchair for when walkin' might be too far."

"So you returned from the casino and helped get the wheelchair into his room."

"Yes, sir . . . uh . . . Gus. And when Mr. T was getting ready for bed I cleaned Willie's litter-box and gave him fresh food 'n water. Willie has to have somethin' in his dish to get through the night so he won't wake Mr. T. I petted him some. Willie is always happy to see us come in."

"What else can you think of that Mr. Townsend did that night?"

Willie stood and looked out the window, thinking. Then he filled a bottle of water. "I'll be right back. I see the birds are lookin' for their water. It dries up near bout every day, and then some."

Estrada stood at the door and watched Joel pour water into a pie dish that sat on a stump.

Back inside, Joel said, "All I can think of is . . . Mr. T went into the bathroom and washed up. I heard him brush his teeth. Then he went into his bedroom and came out in his jamas and robe. He was gonna watch a little TV before goin' to bed."

"Did he seem ill at that time?"

"No, sir . . . Gus . . . not at all. He was lively and enjoyed petting Willie."

"Did you see him eat or drink anything else, after he got home?"

Joel paused before answering. "I didn't see anything. I think he takes pills for somethin', maybe blood pressures, but I didn't see. Other times I seen him take pills he kep' in the bathroom."

"And you left after you finished feeding Willie?"

"Yes, sir. I said goodnight and I'd see him again in the morn'n."

"You have your own key?"

"Yes. Mr. T gave me one. He said he might not always be up or be in the apartment, and I should just hep mysef and come in. He trusted me."

"Joel, I think you should know that preliminary tests show the presence of strychnine in Mr. Townsend's blood. It may have gotten into his pills somehow. Some places use it for rat poison. Mr. Townsend had cocoa and his cup is at the forensics lab now."

"Oh no." Joel felt implicated; fingers would point to him. He knew the poison was stored in a utility closet near the dining room. Pests were always a problem anywhere that there was a restaurant. His breath stuck in his throat. He looked around at his small home; he had felt at peace here for years. He had had a job and he had had Mr. T's and Hannah's friendship, and he had Willie to care for. Now it could all end. Would the police think he had access to rat poison?

"Did you know about the cocoa, Joel?"

"No, sir . . . G . . . Gus."

"Joel, no one is a suspect yet. It's routine to question everyone who had a key or had access to Mr. Townsend's apartment. I can think of at least six or seven people right off. Were you ever aware of Mr. Townsend's arguing with anyone?"

"Oh, no, he was easy-going, and ever-one liked him."

"Joel, would you know who else had a key to his room?"

"Mr. Lopez, the manager, has a master key. Fits every room, all hunerd-and-sixty, plus utility rooms, the kitchen, and all. The front desk has a master. They have to have for emergencies. Maintenance, housekeeping, and caregivers are given a master when they report for duty. They get called all times of day and night. Sometimes to hep people who fall and can't get up theirsevs. Security has to have a master key; sometimes a resident will forget and leave water running. It has happened that when security checked the halls, he has seen water running from under an apartment door."

Estrada raised his eye brows in amazement. "Who's paying for Willie's food and litter now?" Detective Estrada asked.

"Hannah and me, sir. She's the first shift receptionist . . . you probably know."

Yes, pretty legs, Estrada thought. "Well, I want to contribute, sir," Estrada said. "If you are going to call me 'sir,' I'll call you 'sir.' " He fished for a twenty-dollar bill and placed it under a coaster on an end table. He was not in a hurry to leave this tidy and peaceful place. He could not believe for a second that this gentle person would want to kill his patron. Yet, with a key to the room and regular visits there twice daily, and probably the last person to see Mr. Townsend alive, Joel would be a prime suspect. Estrada said, "Thank you Joel. I won't take up any more of your day off." He stood to leave.

"That's okay . . . ." Joel had a hard time calling Estrada 'Gus.' "Every day is a workday in a sense. Most days I go in twice to take care of Willie. Mr. T would want it so. I wonder what will happ'n to Willie."

The contented look Joel had when Detective Estrada arrived had evolved into a worried frown. As he drove out of the dusty driveway, Estrada knew he had just planted another shock for Joel on top of the shock of Mr. Townsend's death. What would Joel have had to gain by doing in Mr. T, as he was called? It would be interesting to learn the provisions of Mr. T's will. Quite interesting. That would be known shortly.

As he drove along Continental Road, Detective Estrada decided to stop off for groceries—put Canyon Grove out of mind for an hour or so. He planned to interrogate Mercedes Salinas next. Her shift was 3:00 in the afternoon to 11:00. He preferred to catch her at work and the later hours would be best, he thought—fewer people around. He would arrive unannounced at 10:30 in the late evening. to question her, and to watch how the shift change went at 11:00.

He bought chicken breasts; he would keep dinner simple and broil them in the oven with a coating of barbecue sauce added the last five minutes. Simmer corn ears to go with it; early corn was in the store now. At home he put away the groceries and checked his mail and email. Then he noticed the telephone trying to get his attention. A message from Detective Collins to call as soon as he got in. Collins answered on the first ring.

"Gus, strychnine has definitely been confirmed in Mr. Townsend's cup with cocoa remains. And from around the apartment, five distinct sets of prints were lifted, not counting Mr. Townsend's. Two sets of prints proved to be the day shift receptionists; one set Joel's; one set Oliver Townsend, Mr. Townsend's nephew . . . and a mystery set. Mr. Townsend's water glass and pill containers in the bathroom had only his prints. The mystery prints were on Mr. Townsend's cocoa box."

"On his cocoa box?"

"Yes."

"I see . . . we'll be busy learning who the mystery set belongs to."

At 10:30 that evening, Detective Estrada signed in at the Canyon Grove reception counter where Mercedes Salinas sat looking at a computer monitor. Estrada could see brightly colored clothing for sale on a web site. Mercedes had seen him come in the door but did not turn her head to look at him. Nor did she greet him.

"Excuse me . . . you are Mercedes Salinas, are you not?"

She looked over at him without answering.

"I want a few minutes of your time for questions about Mr. Townsend's death." Estrada showed his badge, even though by now, she would certainly know who he was.

"But, I'm on duty now," she said. "I have to man the phones, and direct the caregivers."

"That's perfectly okay. I'll work around that. It seems quiet right now."

Mercedes flipped off the web site, pulled a sigh, and turned in her seat to face the detective across the counter.   He saw a second chair in the reception office. "Do you mind, Ms Salinas, if I come around there and sit for a few minutes?"

"Of course not," she shrugged. She scowled as she pulled up the chair and unlatched the half-door for him.

"Ms Salinas, both yours and Hannah Baker's fingerprints were found in Mr. Townsend's apartment. On what occasion did you go in there?" He knew, but did not say, that her prints were found on one of the letters in Mr. Townsend's desk drawer.

"I took packages in sometimes; something he had ordered. And he would ask me to sit a minute," she lied.

"Maggie Smith next door heard yelling one night," Detective Estrada said. "Do you know what that was about?"

"No."

Sitting in the shade of a palo verde tree, Joel thought about Detective Estrada's visit. It had clearly been an official one; that was just the man's job. Estrada hadn't asked Joel how he came to live in Green Valley—unusual. Joel thought well of him for that. Others asked. It was a disguised way of saying that Joel was misplaced. Detective Estrada acted as if it were natural that Joel was there. Was it? Joel mused about how he came to be there.

Two doctors, husband and wife, had brought Joel to Green Valley. They had hired him after first meeting him working in a New Haven, Connecticut hospital. Years back, when kids from the projects were trespassing on railroad tracks, one pushed Joel in front of a train, and Joel lost his left hand. Then, in more recent years, when the hospital was bought by an HMO, and that HMO, not thinking that Joel could possibly do the work that he had been doing for five years, laid him off, the doctors hired Joel directly. They had a large home with extensive grounds, and they all managed quite well with Joel living in their carriage house, watching over the place, tending gardens.

When the doctors retired, they downsized and moved to Green Valley. They had become dependent on Joel and brought him with them, again providing a home for him; this time in their casita. Again, everything went well. Joel did all the yard maintenance and heavy cleaning, even learned to catch snakes with his one hand. He would first have a conversation with the snake, then while the dumb snake was trying to decipher this crazy one-handed man, Joel would grab it right at the neck and drop it over the patio wall into the arroyo. And after the doctors bought Joel a battery-driven golf cart, he did much of the grocery shopping.

When in time both doctors died, their daughter told Joel he would have to go. The house and casita would be sold. With the money he had saved, having never had anything to spend it on, he bought an acre of desert scrub that already had a small mobile home, plumbing, water, and electricity. Used to living alone, he did not mind his existence; found it peaceful. He had learned how to coax water out of the desert soil to make a small pond, and he would sit under the palo verdes to watch animals come to drink and bathe. He wanted for nothing else but a little money for extras.

In time Joel met his neighbors—usually by passing on the sandy road. One day a neighbor told him about Canyon Grove and what a hard time they were having finding a handyman. That's what he was, Joel supposed, a 'handyman.'

He thought back about how he had taken the golf cart to Canyon Grove and had interviewed with Mr. Steve Lopez. The interview had not gone well. Mr. Lopez indicated that Joel couldn't be as capable as he said, even though Joel told him that he could hang wallpaper perfectly. He described a system he had worked out using a board nailed to a post.

Steve was shaking his head *no*, when Mr. T happened by the office door, and glanced in just in time to catch the gist of the interview. Mr. T told Steve that he needed such a man as

Joel to help with this and that including Willie, his cat. So it turned out that Joel went to work for Mr. T and Canyon Grove. The arrangement had worked out just fine. But what would happen to him now? At a time when he most needed help, there was none. So far, he was still going to work and taking care of Willie until those in control decided what to do.

Friday evening, Detectives Estrada and Collins knocked on Hannah Baker's door. Could she give them some time for questions? they asked.

"Of course." Hannah invited them into her small townhome and asked them to take off their jackets and have a seat.

"We have talked to Joel and he says you are helping him with Willie's expenses," Estrada said.

"Yes, I do, but it's not much . . . a few dollars."

Estrada took out his notebook and wrote something.

"While you're doing that," Hannah said, "let me put coffee on for us."

The detectives nodded in agreement. A chill had set in and monsoons, reluctant to clear out, maintained the raw air as a reminder of their power. Hot coffee would hit the spot. Their appreciative glances followed Hannah into the kitchen. From where they sat, they could see her putting the coffee together. She had an interesting, intelligent face that one could look at for a long time without tiring, and a smile Estrada wanted to take home with him, that fronted a quiet, assured attitude. And those legs. Estrada and Collins watched her with the coffee maker. They gave each other a look.

Collins needn't look, Estrada thought. He has a wife to whom he's much attached. Goes home to her every night. But I go home to an empty house. Hannah Baker's the first woman who's not attached—at least he hoped she was not attached—that he'd been drawn to since Gloria moved out.

Hannah returned and placed on the coffee table a tray with mugs of coffee, a creamer, and sugar. "Please help yourself," she said.

"Ms Baker, you know that strychnine was found in Mr. Townsend's blood," Detective Estrada began.

Hannah was nodding her head, yes.

"Strychnine's a lethal poison, used often in commercial establishments for rodent control. We found a small supply of strychnine powder in a Canyon Grove utility closet. We asked Mr. Walters in maintenance, and he confirmed that it was used sparingly from time to time in special safety traps in the kitchen. And that utility closet can be opened only by a master key. We believe two master keys for emergencies are always stored in reception's right-hand drawer."

"That's true," Hannah said.

"Have you missed one of those keys?"

"Well, I haven't checked. No one has asked for one."

"Who has access to that drawer other than you, Ms Salinas, and the night receptionist?"

"Management," Hannah said. "Steve Lopez, whom you've met, and also our bookkeeper, and the personnel manager. They have offices behind reception. But when they're on duty everyone has his own set: the caregivers . . . the nurse."

"We noticed that you keep reception's half-door latched."

"Yes, we do. Before that half-door was installed, some residents would come right in to our tiny work area, sit, and chatter so we couldn't work. Ms Smith, Mr. T's neighbor, whom you've probably met, was a good one for that. Before the half-door was installed, she would sit in reception and yatter. We must be tactful, but she made it difficult. Our half-door and wrap-around counter protect our work area, and the residents can still reach us. The first two shifts are hectic, with many details to take care of, people to assist, people coming and going, and we have to see that all visitors sign in. Often there is a lot of commotion around reception. Some of our residents become restless and pace the hallways, even in the middle of the night; some get confused."

"Is reception ever left unattended?" Estrada asked.

"Rarely. But on third-shift, 11:00 at night to 7:00 in the morning, if a security guard can't come in for some reason, which happened recently for a week when our guard took an emergency family leave, the third-shift receptionist has to put the phones on mobile and walk the extensive halls every hour, checking exit doors to be sure they're locked. Some residents go outside to smoke, and might fail to lock the door when they come back in."

Hannah paused to think about what else was significant.

"When newspapers arrive at four in the morning, the receptionist has to deliver them to the apartments. That can't wait. We leave the papers outside residents' doors . . . you know, in the interior hallway. Some residents, unable to sleep, want their newspaper as soon as it's delivered."

Detective Estrada wrote something in his notebook. "We have to ask everyone this," he said, "did you have occasion to be in Mr. Townsend's apartment?"

"Yes. Joel feeds Willie twice daily and cleans his litter. This means that he has to get here at seven in the morning, work an eight-hour shift, go home, and return at five or six in the afternoon. He can manage that, but since I live a block from Canyon Grove, I walk over sometimes and feed Willie for him. Save him a trip. Mr. T and I were on friendly terms, and he approved "

Estrada was relieved to hear this. He had not been able to get out of mind that Maggie Smith said she had seen Hannah Baker often going and coming from Mr. Townsend's apartment. "Can you think of anyone who had a problem with Mr. Townsend?"

Without hesitation, Hannah said *no*. "Mr. T was admired by all . . . too much so in some cases. Maggie Smith, his neighbor, trailed him around. He tolerated her with kindness, but it was clear that he avoided her when he could."

"Aside from you and Joel, who else had fairly regular access to his room?" Estrada asked.

"Housekeeping. He had weekly service I think. Mrs. Joules has been a housekeeper here for a decade and is trusted. Then there is his nephew, Oliver Townsend. He's terrific about visiting his uncle, usually twice a week. I often see him sign in. He takes Mr. T out to lunch or dinner. I think he has his own key."

In between taking notes, Detective Estrada studied Hannah. She wore no wedding ring. He imagined asking her out to dinner, but sadly, he had to stick to business. Besides, so far, the cause of Mr. Townsend's death had not been resolved. How did he get strychnine?

After the detectives left, Hannah reviewed their questions. She had heard the rumor about poison. Surely, no one at Canyon Grove was capable of such, and who hated Mr. T? No one. Should she have told them that she saw Mercedes and Steve out together? Why would that matter? Why would that have anything to do with Mr. T's death? Except for Mercedes, those with access to Mr. T's room were all long-term trusted employees. Mercedes had been at Canyon Grove only a year or so. Hannah wondered whose fingerprints had matched up with those in Mr. T's apartment. She had found Detective Estrada to be most appealing. His straightforward manner had an underlying kindness about it. But of course—he was on duty.

Steve Lopez had hired Mercedes Salinas for second shift reception when the former receptionist had gotten herself pregnant and had given short notice. Steve didn't like change like that—too risky; employees had to have good social skills required for dealing with a few confused, or even crotchety, residents, and Steve had not sensed such skills in Mercedes. She had been trying to be hired into almost any position at Canyon Grove, and Steve had continued to say there was no opening; people were happy working there and there was almost no employee turnover. Yet, when she confided to Steve that she thought her natural father lived there, a Mr. Raymond Townsend, Steve's ears tuned in. Mr. Townsend—familiarly known as Mr. T—was richer than an Arab king. Steve wasn't sure why, but that could become important.

"For many years my mother worked as maid in the Townsend household," Mercedes had said to Steve, "until she had me to raise and decided to retire. Someone paid for her upkeep. My guess is . . . Mr. Townsend. Mother never revealed my father. She died two years ago, and I decided to try to convince Mr. T, as you call him, that he is it. I know he is richer than Midas, so maybe my efforts will pay off."

Therefore, with his interest peaked, Steve started taking Mercedes around. He told her it had to be a secret that they were dating. Because of the small and personal nature of the retirement home, company policy frowned on such employee relationships. Mercedes had no choice, if she wanted a position at the residence—that was the way it had to be.

Thus installed in her position as second shift receptionist, she began befriending Raymond Townsend—Mr. T, as some called him. The old coot—she didn't really like him, but faking it was easy for her. Her mother had never said anything against him—it was just that he was so rich, and her mother hadn't been. Mr. Townsend had worked hard all his life, but

Mercedes thought only her mother had had to work hard. When he would come by reception, she would smile brightly—a saccharine smile—and say, "Hello, Mr. T. Anything I can help you with?" And if a package came for him, she would make certain to personally deliver it to his apartment. On occasion, she stuck cheerful cards under his door. In return, he wondered about all the attention, but in his dignity tried to ignore it. Until the evening Mercedes knocked on his apartment door.

She stepped in without being asked, and when she stood there awkwardly—out of politeness Mr. Townsend asked her to have a seat. His first thought was that perhaps she had a problem with which she thought he could help.

She did.

"You are my father," she said. "My mother worked for you many years during which time I was born. Mother told me that you were my father." Her mother had said nothing of the sort; however, who would know?

Mr. Townsend, still standing, gaped at her. Incredible. Except when courtesy demanded, he had never even noticed the household staff. He had been gone so much that the late Mrs. Townsend had managed their staff. He had barely ever seen the woman Mercedes said was her mother.

"My dear . . . not at all true," he said, when he caught his breath. "Impossible! You are seriously mistaken. I suggest you leave now, and we will say no more about this. You could lose your job." He opened the door for her, and she slowly pulled herself up out of the chair.

"I know what I'm talking about, and I insist that you admit that you are my father."

He said nothing more as he shut the door on her. My god, he thought, life had been moving along smoothly, and now this.

Steve held Mercedes' arm as they took hesitant steps over loose rocks along Madeira Canyon trail. They wore hiking boots and jackets for the chilly altitude and lush green shade of the Canyon. The trail was narrow and most of the time they climbed with Steve leading, watching for snakes, and Mercedes trailing. The hike was taxing for two people who didn't hike regularly, but a tasty lunch of tuna salad sandwiches, chips and beer, followed by hot coffee, awaited them back at the picnic table. Mercedes had hurriedly pulled together the lunch, and before Steve had picked her up, he had stopped for beer. They needed to talk, he had said, but it would have to wait until they were down from the climb. Not used to the altitude, they panted as they climbed.

Back at the picnic table they munched on sandwiches while Steve took the opportunity to reaffirm their situation. "You and I must not be seen together. The less we give people to talk about the better. And, as I've said before, inter-company dating is against company policy."

Mercedes did not say this to Steve, but she wanted to be seen with him. She had flamed off her last boyfriend, and men her age were in short supply in Green Valley. She registered her disappointment. Patience, Steve had said. They had to be patient.

She had already told him about Mr. T's reaction to her claim. It did not sound good, Steve thought, and he suggested she back off a bit; he did not want to receive a complaint and to have to terminate her employment.

"But I want to threaten Mr. T with DNA testing."

"But what if it proves he couldn't be your father?" Steve asked.

"I'll take that chance. If he is my father I could stand to profit from his estate, and he's already at least ninety. Besides, he might come around without DNA testing, not wanting the embarrassment of publicity."

"Hmmm, I'll have to think about that," Steve said. "As it stands now, he'll probably leave everything to his nephew. Meanwhile, I have to get back to work, and you're due there at three, as you know."

"Will I see you tonight?" Mercedes asked.

"I don't know . . . I haven't been home long enough lately to catch up on things, and get some sleep." Truth was—if she was not Mr. T's daughter, maybe she was not worth all the trouble; he would see.

On duty that evening, Mercedes wrote the letter, unsigned—Mr. T would know it was from her—and slipped it under his door. The next night, when she was on duty, he handed her his reply, unsigned. These were the letter and letter copy that Detective Estrada had found in Mr. Townsend's drawer.

Maggie Smith sat in the Canyon Grove dining room fingering her spoon, gazing off across the room at the pianist. The jazz performer was capable, but Maggie wasn't paying attention. She had recently lost a pet project—that of winning Mr. T—"Ray"—she called him, and she was considering that loss. Whenever she caught him sitting in the dining room, she would greet him as a close companion—after all, he lived in the apartment next to hers. Hadn't that conferred rights? The other women would look at her with envy. Old enough to know better, Maggie thought, they all still wanted a man. And Maggie had one. At least that's what it looked like to outsiders. True, Ray never asked her to dinner, nor in for a glass of wine, but she would knock and invite herself into his apartment from time to time, and sometimes their neighbors would see her coming out. Good.

Actually losing Ray had been her own fault. The time had come when she could no longer tolerate his clear lack of interest. Enough time had elapsed since she had started her project, and the time had come to wrap it up. Before they had installed reception's half-door, Maggie would step in, take a seat and chat; the receptionists were so friendly. From this, she had learned that a master key, one that fit every door in the residence, was kept in a right-hand top drawer. She had seen the receptionist give it to a plumber. And, Maggie had found out from her nightly wanderings, that sometimes when there was no security guard, the receptionist would have to leave the reception kiosk every hour to make the rounds, and also to deliver newspapers when they arrived about four in the morning.

Maggie had always hated her front window that looked into the hallway; had to keep the blinds closed for privacy, but now that window would prove itself valuable. Through that window she would occasionally hear the security guard, or receptionist, make rounds every hour from eleven at night until seven in the morning. One night when Maggie knew the regular security guard was out sick, and the third-shift receptionist, Ellie, was making the rounds, Maggie listened for Ellie to pass by.

When she was sure that Ellie was out of sight around the curved hallway, Maggie rushed down the hall in the opposite direction to the reception kiosk and helped herself to a master key. There were two, so maybe one wouldn't be missed right away. She could easily find an opportunity to put it back later. Besides, even if the key was missed, no one would know that she had it.

She started on her way around one of the interior hallways. She passed Ellie coming from the other direction. That was okay—Ellie, used to seeing Maggie walking at night, said hello, and kept on going. When Maggie reached the opposite side of that four-leaf-clover, near the kitchen, she used the master key and opened the storage room. She had plenty of time—Ellie wouldn't be back that way for another hour. With her nosy nature poking into everything, Maggie had seen into this storage room before, and knew that rat poison was kept there. It took a minute to find what she was looking for, and there it was on a shelf—rat poison—with the graphic of skull and crossbones. She opened the box expecting pellets, but it was a greyish powder. They must mix it with a bit of food that rats go for, she thought. Then she realized, thinking about Ray's hot chocolate, that powder was probably better than pellets. She could mix this gray powder right in with his cocoa; wouldn't have to crush it. She poured some of the powder into a vinyl bag she had thought to bring. The filched master key would serve a dual purpose, she mused: the next time Ray went out to dinner, she would enter his apartment and doctor his cocoa. No need to worry about having the key; there was no way anyone could know that she had it.

"The lab confirmed traces of strychnine in Mr. Townsend's box of hot cocoa." Detective Collins relayed this information to Detective Estrada over the phone.

"Proves our suspicions," said Estrada. "Thinking about the fingerprints we found on that cocoa box, that so far have not been identified . . . we will have to fingerprint more employees . . . those we've missed: caregivers, the laundress, maintenance people, third-shift employees, the activity director. Some of them will be hard to contact, as they work rotating shifts."

Estrada clicked off the phone and sat a while longer in Mr. Townsend's apartment, petting and talking to Willie. "I'm sorry for you, Willie, I know you are lonely. I know you have seen a lot, and I wish you could tell me what has gone on here." He continued to sit, expecting the apartment to talk to him in some way—tell him who had wanted Mr. Townsend dead. Thought experiments had proved useful on other cases—just sitting thinking, saying to himself, what if? followed by different outcomes. Of those whose fingerprints had been identified in the apartment, only Joel had had the most opportunity. Mercedes Salinas' prints, though she may have been thinking black mail, were found only on one chair arm and on her letter to Mr. Townsend. Hannah Baker's had been found only on Willie's dish and on a couple of empty cat food cans. (Detective Estrada had relaxed an entire muscle group after receiving that information.) Oliver Townsend's prints were just on a chair arm. Joel's were everywhere, which was normal considering all he did for Mr. Townsend. Except for Mr. Townsend's and a mystery set, no other prints were found on the cocoa can.

Enough time spent sitting there. He said goodbye to Willie, gave him a last stroke, and stepped out into the hallway. Just as he locked Mr. Townsend's door, Maggie Smith came out of her adjacent apartment. Oh, no, he thought, here comes Betty Davis.

"Sleuthing again, I see," Maggie Smith said brightly. "I'll miss Ray." Her unnatural smile spread from ear to ear.

"Did you and Mr. Townsend visit often?" Estrada asked.

"Oh, yes . . . he and I were close," she fibbed.

While they walked toward reception, Detective Estrada tried to avoid her face as Maggie kept beaming at him. She doesn't seem to really mind the loss of Mr. Townsend, the detective thought. She acts as cheerful and as happy as can be. How convenient for her that I often bump into her. Too bad it isn't Hannah Baker that I bump into. When he reached his car, he dialed Detective Collins.

"We should fingerprint Maggie Smith," Estrada said. "We have to make up some kind of story . . . tell her anything . . . that all the residents have to be checked. She'll probably love the attention."

"Looks like you will escape further police interest," Steve said to Mercedes. "But that letter you wrote to Mr. T could really have gotten you into deep trouble. It's a good thing your prints could not be found anywhere else in his apartment. You can kiss that connection goodbye, and don't do any other stupid thing while you're working here . . . else you won't have a job. Since they don't know yet who had the poison, you're still a suspect as we all are."

"I know . . . I'm sorry," Mercedes said. "Will you come over tonight? We haven't had time together lately."

"True," he said, "but with all that's been going on, all the stressful coming and going of detectives, I need a couple of quiet nights at home. Now they tell me they want to fingerprint some of the residents. That's just what we need for business . . . as if a poisoning wasn't enough."

"Good morning, Ms Smith, may we come in?" asked Detective Estrada.

Maggie was thrilled and all smiles until she saw the handcuffs that Detective Collins did not try to conceal. Estrada hadn't meant it as a question either, and he gently pushed his way into Maggie's apartment. Collins shut the door behind them. Estrada quoted the Miranda warning to Maggie and said, "Ms Maggie Smith, we are taking you in for further questioning. Your prints were found on Mr. Townsend's cocoa box."

"But I have made cocoa for him," she lied. She stepped back to gain distance from the detectives.

"Well, that may be, but how do you explain your prints on the rat poison box in the utility room? And how will you explain the master key that I think we will find in your apartment?"

Maggie looked confused. Had she really forgotten to put back that blasted key?

"We don't want to have to handcuff you, Ms Smith. I hope you will walk out with us quietly, smiling, so as to not cause unnecessary attention and suspicion."

Betty Davis, not known for her smiles, would have been amused at the one Maggie managed on the way out to the detectives' car. Hannah felt sad as she saw them leave, though she pretended not to notice. Steve could see them from his open doorway. He did not pretend not to notice; he was relieved. Maybe the staff would be left alone now.

Joel continued to care for Willie. No decision had been made about Willie's disposition. Hannah continued to help Joel sometimes with money for cat food, and as well, she often fed Willie in the evening so Joel wouldn't have to make that second trip back. Steve Lopez was considering letting Joel go. After all, it was Mr. Townsend who had needed Joel's help the most. Canyon Grove could get along without Joel's one-handed work. Steve would decide about this after they closed Mr. Townsend's apartment, and after his nephew had dispersed the contents, and after Willie's removal had been decided. He didn't want to be too quick and obvious about letting Joel go. Joel was too well liked.

There could have been a sad ending: that Joel was laid off and, unable to find another job, had barely enough money on which to subsist, and that Willie was taken to the Animal League, and that Maggie Smith was executed, and that

Mercedes Salinas was laid off; Steve Lopez tired of her, and that Detective Estrada continued his lonely existence, and that Hannah Baker continued hers. But that's not what happened. None of it.

What really happened, was that one afternoon, when he knew Joel would be home, Detective Estrada knocked on his door. Joel welcomed the detective, happy to see him.

"Joel, I have just come from the reading of Mr. Townsend's Will, and Joel, I have something most important to tell you."

"Yes, sir, uh . . . , Gus." Joel wore a puzzled—perhaps even anxious look. Could a Will get him in trouble somehow?

"Joel, you're a wealthy man."

After this declaration, Detective Estrada took a long pause to determine whether Joel, looking perplexed, understood.

"In appreciation for all your kindness over the years, Mr. T left you a fortune. Joel, you can buy a house. You can buy a house anywhere you want. You can buy a house in Manhattan if you want to. Heck, you can buy a penthouse with a floor for you and a floor for Willie." In his delight over conveying happy information, Detective Estrada flourished with exaggeration. "That's part of the bargain, though . . . if anything happened to him, Mr. T wanted you to take Willie. Seeing as how you and Willie care for each other, I don't think that's going to be a barrier."

Joel, shock freezing his face, twisted his fingers together over and over. If he had been wearing a hearing aide, he would have twisted that. He seemed not to comprehend. Was Gus playing a joke on him?

Joel, do you understand what I'm saying to you?" Detective Estrada asked with emphasis. "Mr. Townsend's Will was read today . . . I had an interest in being at the reading. Mr. Townsend left you a fortune. I'm referring to money, Joel!"

I won't trouble you with Joel's problems adjusting to his new financial position. It took months. Except for Willie's needs, Joel was still afraid to spend a penny. And when word about Mr. T's Will got around Canyon Grove, Joel almost hated to go in because of the attention he received. People seemed to step back when they saw him approaching. Steve Lopez was afraid to terminate Joel now, and looked at him with renewed respect, almost stuttering when he spoke to him. Steve couldn't believe how wealthy one hand could become. Mercedes made unnecessary fusses over him. Hannah treated him the same as ever. Oliver Townsend didn't at all mind the wealth his uncle had left Joel. There was plenty to go around and he had seen over the years how necessary, and how kind, Joel had been to his uncle. In fact, the three of them had had numerous dinners together.

Joel loved his acre and mobile home and palo verde trees, but he knew it wouldn't be good for Willie. Willie couldn't be allowed to roam the desert. Giant owls made light snacks out of cats, and the mobile home was so small. Joel would need a new home, one that would also be good for Willie.

Detective Estrada had already guessed as much, as had Hannah. Estrada asked Joel and Hannah out to dinner to discuss this situation. Mr. Townsend's apartment was being closed, and soon Joel had to remove Willie. Joel said that if he had his druthers, and had enough money, he wanted to move back to New England. He had a sister there, who wrote to him. Maybe he could help her some. He missed having a little garden. And he missed dirt. And grass. And if he had an acre back there, he could have his garden, and Willie could go out a little.

"Joel, you can buy half of New England if you've a mind. I'm exaggerating a bit, Joel, but you have more than plenty for an acre. Hannah and I will come up and help you, if you'll let us. Won't we Hannah?"

(And they did.)

Not long after that dinner, Detective Estrada asked Ms Hannah Baker to a quiet dinner to "discuss how to help Joel," he said. Whatever the reason, Hannah looked forward to the evening. Estrada began planning menus when he would cook for her. She looked forward to seeing him. Joel looked forward to their trip north to help him buy his acre.

I'm not forgetting Maggie Smith. She got life in an institution. The judge wouldn't give her the chair. She was too old and confused. Thought she was Betty Davis.

About Shirley Mason

During a seventeen-year career as programmer analyst, Shirley Mason wrote and enhanced, software systems for computer installations in Connecticut and New York. Through those years there wasn't adequate time to raise children, paint, and write. So to keep thinking about words and putting one here, and putting another there, she wrote limericks in stop-and-go traffic. Long hours and long commutes did not allow her to take writing seriously until the end of all that commuting. These days, she writes, and in between that, she paints, and in between that she is a silversmith.

And don't forget her cat Sophie.

Write to her. Slarsen22@aol.com